Penguin Crime Fiction
Editor: Julian Symons
Love in Amsterdam

Nicolas Freeling was born in London in 1927 and spent
his childhood in France. Before taking up writing he
worked for many years in hotels and restaurants, and
from their back doors got to know a good deal of Europe.
When *Love in Amsterdam*, his first novel, was published
in 1962 he stopped cooking other people's dinners and
went back to Holland. His second and third novels,
Because of the Cats and *Gun Before Butter* were
published in 1963. They have all been published in
Penguins, as well as *Valparaiso*, *The Dresden Green*,
The King of the Rainy Country, *Criminal Conversation*,
Tsing Boum and *Strike Out Where Not Applicable*. His
latest books are *The Cook Book* and *A Long Silence*.

Double-Barrel, *Because of the Cats*, *Love in Amsterdam*
and *King of the Rainy Country* are all available in
Penguins in the U.S.A.

Love In Amsterdam

Nicolas Freeling

Penguin Books

Penguin Books Ltd, Harmondsworth,
Middlesex, England
Penguin Books Inc., 7110 Ambassador Road,
Baltimore, Maryland 21207, U.S.A.
Penguin Books Australia Ltd, Ringwood,
Victoria, Australia
Penguin Books Canada Ltd, 41 Steelcase Road West,
Markham, Ontario, Canada
Penguin Books (N.Z.) Ltd, 182–190 Wairau Road,
Auckland 10, New Zealand

First published in the United States by Harper & Row,
Publishers, Inc., New York, 1962
Published by Penguin Books Inc. by arrangement with
Harper & Row, Publishers, Inc.
First published in Great Britain by Victor Gollancz 1962
Published in Penguin Books 1965
Reprinted 1969, 1975
Copyright © Nicolas Freeling, 1962

Made and printed in Great Britain by
Hazell Watson & Viney Ltd,
Aylesbury, Bucks
Set in Linotype Times

Contents

Contents

Part One

The House in the Josef Israelskade

The man paced up and down the cell. It was a large cell, he thought, and a good one; clean and bright. Though he had done so several times before, he looked at the furniture with careful interest. He did not know why he should be interested. 'It's that I have nothing to do,' he thought; and then, 'That's not so, either.' He was always interested in such things, wherever he was. 'Waste nothing,' he said aloud, and then again, not aloud. It didn't do to talk out loud. Not that the warders minded; you could stand on your head all day without bothering them in the slightest, but some damn psychiatrist might have told them to write down anything he did, and infer something silly from it. Pretty silly, he thought; all men talk to themselves aloud; they do a lot more, and without anybody calling the witchdoctor. They listen to their own voices, they conduct imaginary orchestras while listening to the gramophone. 'They look at their faces in the glass,' he thought; ' "You're a smart son of a bitch," they say – aloud. Means nothing; tension. Nervous trick, like scratching, or picking your nose. Millionaire plans take-over – secretary enters, finds great man picking his nose. "I meant no disrespect, Sir Roderick." '

The cement walls were plastered and painted a darkish cream up to waist height. Then came a narrow green stripe. 'What kind of green is that? Leaf green? What Elsie de Wolfe called lamp-post and park-bench green.' The top half of the walls and the ceiling were a paler cream. Darkest – but still cream – was the heavy steel door. Damn cream. 'Am I a cheese merchant? Cheese mite,' he decided. The ceiling was high, with a shaded neon tube. He counted the steel knobs in the door; nine rows of four, and in the middle row the two inner knobs are missing, because of the little panel. 'They don't seem to use that panel; they always open the door; keys, bolts. Not any real trouble – purely automatic movements. Keys don't tire them or worry them any more; they can find any one by touch, and the time spent is all automatically allowed for. At home they are probably surprised at opening doors so easily.' The window was ribbed glass, and pretty dirty, but how do you make a good job of cleaning ribbed glass with bars outside? Inside there was plenty more cream. The folding bed, the hot-water pipes, the little corner cupboard, the three coat-hooks, the waist-high wooden screen round the lavatory bucket.

On the wall hung a little rack for your knife, fork and spoon, a typewritten list of rules covered in plastic, and a vaguely biblical picture. This showed a bearded shepherd, gazing dramatically at a lot of splashy stars and surrounded by a rocky science-fiction landscape. Presented by the *Christelijke Vereniging* of something in small print – some Prisoners' Aid affair with worthy intentions. He had a good-sized glass, too; he stopped polar-bearing and stared in it. The face looked a bit tatty and bloodshot; he looked with detachment, and thought the face badly put together, not well balanced. 'Can't help it, got to live with it. Hair needs cutting too.'

He turned back to the table, which gave him especial pleasure. Good, big, solid table, nice and smooth, good height. It was varnished a particular shade of yellow ochre that was somehow familiar, and as he stared he knew why. Convents varnished their furniture that colour. Now why should jails and convents share a liking for exactly that rather hideous shade? Perhaps because it did look clean and bright, and neither jails nor convents are very attached to beauty. Not their job. The table was a good one anyway and that gave him pleasure. Not important, but perhaps it would become important. The wood was hard, and the legs solid and level; there was room for everything; one could work at this table, if one had paper and a pen. He put a folded blanket on his chair, sat at the table and started rolling a cigarette. Half-zwaar shag; he was getting quite to like it.

Elsa was dead. He had thought it all over many times in the two weeks that he had sat locked up. It was in a way a good thing, since Elsa living was a constant menace to him. The more ridiculous that Elsa dead should also be a menace. Typical of her, certainly. It ought not to affect him, except to content him that the one thing that had ever come between Sophia and himself was now gone. But it was affecting him, forcibly.

The police were not in the least concerned that he had neither killed Elsa nor ever had such an idea. They had found her killed, and it was their job to find somebody who had probably killed her. He had been sitting there staring at them. Elsa dead meant to them 'Find somebody to answer for it'. It didn't worry them that they had no proof; they reasoned that the truth would show itself under gentle but steady, ceaseless prodding, which they were good at. A chess problem, no more. White to move and mate in three. They probably didn't believe that he really had killed her. He was going to supply what they needed, a reasonable solution to a criminal problem. To them, it was only a problem; and he was just part of it.

He was sorry that he could not feel sorry for Elsa's death. He felt sorry for the anxiety and strain for Sophia, but she was his wife. One thing Elsa had never been. She would have enjoyed his being in a hole, and Sophia anxious. She liked him tense and strained, and she had detested Sophia. But simply for the pleasure of pestering him, and causing Sophia pain, she would hardly have gone so far. Not so far as to put four pistol bullets into her own stomach. Otherwise, he would not for a moment have put it past her – to arrange this to look like him. She blossomed on dramas and scenes, loved upheavals, denouncements, tremendous rages, weeping reconciliations. That kind of thing was her daily bread and butter. She would be capable of a most intricate and careful scheme just to get him embroiled with his own wife. She had never forgiven Sophia, nor had Sophia ever forgiven her. When it came to murder, Sophia had a lot stronger motives than he had.

Had she done it herself? Could it be possible? Suppose she had an incurable disease, leukaemia or so. Revenge suicide, like dear old Rebecca. Whatever had happened, she had succeeded in interfering drastically with his life even after all these years. She had seriously damaged his career, nearly wrecked his marriage, and now she'd got him in jail, and he had a good chance of staying there a lifetime. He had loved her once. She had illuminated his life for many years; she had been his friend and she was part of his life as the past is always part of the present. Influencing decision, colouring opinion. *L'ombre de la jeune fille en fleur*. Life should still have Elsa in it, and without his hating her; he had only hated her a few months. He had despised her, pitied her, spat on her, desired her (still sometimes), laughed at memories of her, not loved her. Not loving he had had no need to hate. And now she was dead; victim, he had no doubt at all, of one of her involved little treacheries. She was never happy unless her left hand were deceiving her right.

He had been at home; it was nearly midnight and in half an hour he should have been in bed, but he was still drinking the last lukewarm cup of coffee. It was very still, and outside on the Fonteinlaan there was only the odd car swishing away into the distance until one heard again the friendly drip and patter of the rain that had gone on, almost continuously, nearly a week now. He was just sitting idly when the buzzer went. They had no speakbox; there was no real need on the first floor and he disliked them anyway. Like a telephone, an invasion of his home. Sophia had answered the buzzer.

She came back looking annoyed, and he heard strange footsteps. He looked at her, a little ruffled.

'Police.'

'What on earth do they want?'

10

As he went out he changed his frown to the slight smile that was his everyday, business face. Putting on his face. Only Sophia saw his real face.

Outside were the usual pair of comedians. They stood quietly and had taken their caps off. Ordinary Haarlem policemen in short leather jackets; car patrol.

'What's up?' he asked.

The first scratched his hair with his cap. 'Don't really know. Seems you're wanted down at the bureau, that's all.'

'This time of night?'

'Night or day, we never have any peace,' said the second, grinning.

'Oh well. I was just going to bed. I have to work in the morning.'

'Maybe you won't need to work in the morning.'

He didn't like that. 'Why, have I won a football pool?' he joked. They both laughed heartily. Sophia wore the face with which she fought trouble. 'A quiet, wise face,' he thought with love, 'and when there is trouble a ferocious fighter.'

'Don't forget the cigarettes,' she said. 'I'm going to bed. I hope you won't be late.'

She didn't like it either, he saw. She kissed him warmly, with a hard hug; his nerves twanged in his stomach with love for her.

Outside, the two lummels were staring at the coat-rack.

'Better take your raincoat; it's still raining.' The coat was still damp.

'And your hat,' said the other helpfully, holding it out. He wondered why the hell they should be worried about his hat.

They had the usual little black Volkswagen. It did not head for the nearer bureau in Heemstede, but back towards town, along the Dreef and into the Houtplein, up to the central bureau off the Grote Markt. It was still raining gently, persisting out of a cool, fresh, clouded sky.

'What is all this?' He could not help asking, guessing they did not know.

'Do we know?' The one at the back was lounging sideways and chewing a rubber band. He had been waved in beside the driver. 'We like to sit and drink coffee too.'

'Couldn't offer you any,' he joked, 'drunk it all myself.' He lit a cigarette as the driver shifted gears smoothly and made a left turn into the Smedestraat. They stopped outside the bureau, an old-fashioned, crowded-looking and messy building. A brigadier looked up vaguely as they came in, and nodded to the patrol crew. 'Good evening,' said Martin.

'Good evening to you. Mind coming in here?'

It was a little office, where a youngish man sat writing at a desk; the lamp made a cheerful pool of light. The man stood up and held out his hand. 'Van der Valk.' He repeated his name automatically and sat in the chair offered, a hard wooden chair with arms and a tatty seat cushion.

Van der Valk needed a shave, looked tired, and was stabbing out a cigarette with abrupt jerks of his forearm.

'I am an inspector of the *Amsterdamse recherche*,' he said calmly, 'and I'm sorry to get you out so late. It is important however – wouldn't be this late myself if it wasn't – and we think you can tell us the answers to various things that aren't clear.'

The man had tiny nervous compulsions; one was to rub the side of his nose with his forefinger. Martin listened with his eyebrows high and no idea at all what was coming. Van der Valk lit a cigarette without looking at it and fanned the smoke away from his face; he took a fresh sheet of paper and wrote a line at the top.

'Remember last night?'

'Yes. I suppose I might miss a few details.'

'What about, say, between nine and ten, and give the details just as you recall them.'

'I was taking a walk round about then. I'd been to the cinema; it always gives me a headache. Wasn't a bad film; gave me some ideas. When I'm like that, been in a stuffy atmosphere and strained my eyes, I like to walk; it rests me.'

12

The man nodded and wrote a couple of lines.

'Where did you walk? Give me the itinerary if you can.'

'Down over the Frederiksplein, by the brewery, Van Wou-straat, down into Zuid as far as the Apollolaan, back along Ceintuurbaan to the Museumplein where I'd left my car that afternoon.'

'Long walk. Raining pretty hard then too.'

'I like walking in the rain,' said Martin flatly.

Van der Valk looked up. 'I'm not saying it isn't so,' he said peacefully. 'I'm just establishing a picture. Go across the bridge at the Josef Israelskade?'

'No, I went along to that pleasure-palace affair on the corner.'

The man nodded, satisfied. 'What time would that have been, about? That you were there, could you say?'

'Don't know; about a quarter to ten maybe, give or take. Who's dead?' he joked.

Van der Valk did not look up; he was writing slowly, taking pains. 'We'll come to it in a minute,' he said calmly. 'Do you know a woman named Elsa de Charmoy?'

Martin felt he was supposed to look surprised. He was sure he did look surprised.

'Certainly I do.'

'Well?'

'Very well, though I've scarcely seen her in the last – five years, say.'

'How well would that be?'

'Seven years ago, as well as you can get. What do you want me to say? It's a personal affair.'

Van der Valk's eyes crinkled with something like amusement. 'Personal affair for me too, *jongen*. I'm investigating her death.'

Very shocked, Martin took a minute to absorb this. He felt automatically for a cigarette and the policeman pushed his forward. Lady Blanche. He took one.

'How did she die?'

'Someone shot her. Four times. Between nine-thirty and ten.'

'You mean you think I shot her?'

'Don't think anything at all. Trying to find out what I know. For instance, that you know where she lived.'

'I've no idea, but I see what you're getting at. In Zuid somewhere, but she'd moved since I knew her. She left her husband, or he left her – I don't know exactly.'

Van der Valk puffed at his cigarette. 'She lived in a flat on the Josef Israelskade.'

He stood up, walked over to the door, opened it and said, 'Hey.' Martin did not turn round, and heard a mutter. Van der Valk came back and sat meditating.

'Stand up a moment, do you mind? Put your hat on. That's right; look, it's not a gag, but to get something clear. Stand over there by the window; put your hands in your pockets; imagine you're in the street and it's raining.'

'Identity parade?'

'Yes, but it doesn't trap you or incriminate you. You've said frankly that you were in the Josef Israels.'

A uniformed policeman came into the room; he leaned against the door and studied a self-conscious Martin for a moment.

'Not enough light.'

Van der Valk tilted the shade on his reading lamp; Martin blinked and frowned.

The policeman nodded, leisurely.

'Quite sure?' asked Van der Valk sharply.

'No doubt at all.' He had a powerful Amsterdam accent.

The door shut behind him. Martin took off his hat. 'Now tell,' he said.

'About twenty to ten some old woman phoned the police; said there was a man loitering suspiciously by the canal. All nonsense of course – old women get men on the brain – but the bureau told a man on a bike to pass by. Remember seeing him?'

'Why would I notice him?'

14

Van der Valk nodded; that was reasonable. 'That's the chap I just had in. He remembers you; says you weren't loitering; more strolling, staring at the water, up at the lighted windows. That right?' He grinned; Martin grinned back, rather helplessly.

'I dare say.'

'Door or so from Madame de Charmoy's house?'

Helpless slid towards hopeless. He neither knew nor cared where Elsa lived. Who would believe that? Not this geyser, nor Sophia.

'Nobody takes this loitering lark seriously; old women window-peeping. It's just that you were there.'

'Yes.'

Van der Valk opened a desk drawer and came up with a pistol. Mauser seven six five; a beauty.

'Ever see it before?'

'I gave it her.' Whore, he thought bitterly.

'Where d'you get it?'

'In wartime, off a German. For a few cigarettes. As usual.'

Van der Valk nodded again. Stop nodding like a bloody cuckoo-clock, thought Martin, unreasonably.

'Was she shot with that?'

'Why d'you give it her?'

'I gave her anything I thought would amuse her.'

'This time it didn't amuse her much.' He wrote a line or two more and then got up.

'Why?' asked Martin suddenly.

'Why? I don't know why. Don't want to know much. Leave that to the psycho-research geyser. I want to know who.' His voice was tired and irritable. 'Come on, *jongen,* bedtime. Tomorrow we go to Amsterdam and talk it all over. Right now I've got to lock you up.'

'Poor Sophia,' thought Martin. He did not think, 'Poor Elsa.' But just before he slept he thought, 'Yes, poor Elsa.'

They let him sleep till late; it was nearly nine before he was

15

dressed. They let him hang about in the guard office, where an old policeman sat stolidly with a pipe, instead of keeping him locked in the grim little cell. The old gentleman, his face a compendium of the human mind and human follies, did not speak much, and not at all about dead women; he blew a smoke ring, and said, 'Patience is what you need most of, here. Play chess?'

'Yes; not very well.'

'Think of it that way.'

He got a big tin mug of good hot tea, and bread-and-marge with gingercake; he was surprised to find himself hungry. It was ten when the door opened for Van der Valk, rested and grinning. He carried an overnight bag, which he gave Martin.

'You've seen my wife?'

'Explained what I could; told her not to be nervous.'

'Not to be nervous!' thought Martin. Sophia was nervous of a cockroach, but not frightened of the whole Russian army.

She had thought of everything; a pen and paper, the salt liquorice he liked and cigarettes, clean underclothes and washing things, aspirin and eau-de-cologne and some snapshots: Sophia's wise face. He was grateful to Van der Valk. They went out to a little Volkswagen just like the one last night. Van der Valk drove; a uniformed policeman sat in the back, apparently asleep.

The sun shone cleanly on rain-washed streets; all the housewives in the Amsterdamse Buurt seemed to be cleaning their windows. Nobody spoke till they were nearly past the Phoenix factory in Halfweg, with its famous advertisement for packing-cases. 'Want a crate, a box, a container?' thought Martin. 'Want any coffins?'

'I'm in charge of this for a while,' said Van der Valk suddenly, ''till it gets interesting, probably, and complex. You need not worry about the examining magistrate; we haven't decided to charge you. Understand?' Then they were sliding through the streets which seem fuller of gay screeching children than any other streets; shops full of washing machines and endive and sausage; fat *tantes* waddling with shopping bags, and salesmen with bright young faces, briefcases full of confidence and sandwiches, and Fiat Multiplas. Very suddenly they were in the Ferdinand Bolstraat and a second later walking into the police bureau.

The office was like the one in Haarlem but larger; there were two desks and an older, sourer man than Van der Valk was standing trying to stuff papers into a briefcase that would not hold them all.

"Lo Henk.'

"Lo Piet. What you got?'

'Bang-bang in Josef Israels. Woman. What you doing there?'

'Got to go up to the Singel,' with deep gloom, 'and then pass in that file about the hire purchase fraud; the state police want it. And I'll get asked again about that boy on the bike who snatches bags. If I catch that little stinker I'll kick his bottom so hard he'll never face a bike again.' Henk nodded in a friendly way to Martin.

'Mornin'.'

'Mornin'.'

"Bye.' He was gone. Van der Valk shut the window an inch or so and sat down with a sigh of hope. He threw two ballpoints in the wastepaper basket and fussed till he was comfortable. When he was settled he looked levelly at Martin, serious now; a quiet, intelligent man, good at his job.

'Okay, now here's what we've got. Man who lives below Mrs de Charmoy — sorry not Mrs, Miss — is manager of an insurance company, not married, eats out mostly, not at home much. He knows a few of the regular visitors but never paid much heed. That night he's at home. He has a hobby, childish like all business men — one of these high-fidelity maniacs, got a radio diploma. He was playing about with some new gadget he'd just got. Heard a noise, funny noise, like someone breaking up firewood he says, but too quick and regular. That's shots of course. Immediately afterwards someone running, running quickly down stairs. "Immediately" meaning one or two minutes, perhaps. Front door bangs; quiet. Didn't think much, walks out on landing, listens, all still, walks back again. Half an hour later thinks funny. Uneasy, he says. Turns radio off. Turns it on again. Fiddles about, makes up his mind and goes upstairs, rehearsing little speech. "Sorry, Mevrouw; ah, please don't think me inquisitive, it's just that blah blah." No answer to door. Thinks queer, goes down again scratching head, puzzled a bit. All instinct to forget about it, but got some imagination and a bit of a bloodhound; been a claims adjuster in his time, you see. Said it kept echoing in his head – he thought the footsteps peculiar too; hurried. Rings doorbell to Mevrouw's flat, no answer still; worries. Puts on hat and coat; comes here; catches me, just going home as luck would have it. I went and opened the door because I didn't like the story either. Found her.' He paused to light a cigarette.

Martin realized that he had cramped into a hard knot and undid it with a jerk. Surreptitiously he wiped his hand on his trousers. Van der Valk went on as calm as a news announcer.

'I got everything photo'd. Nothing disturbed and nothing taken. I got hold of the agent who'd seen you in the street. Then I found this.'

'This' was an envelope.

'In the writing desk. I went there first because after she was shot she crawled a way towards it, as though she wanted something there. Heaps of stuff I haven't had time to go through, but photos one always goes for first. Have a look.'

Martin had a look. Snapshots. He recognized them all – they were eight or nine years old – except one, which seemed recent. He was standing in the street – looked like the Kalverstraat – gazing open-mouthed in a shop window, looking extraordinarily stupid.

'Candid camera,' said Van der Valk with a laugh.

'I've never seen it or knew it existed. I don't know how she got it.'

'I could see that,' grinning. 'You looked disgusted. Know the others?'

18

'Yes. They're from the time that we were together.'

'The agent recognized it straight away. Said: "That's the geyser in the street." I showed him just to see if we were going to be that lucky. Stroke of luck that it was the same pose, so to speak: in the street and sort of absent-minded expression. Person's not easy to identify when seen in different surroundings. Thing was to find out who it was. Easy. Everything's easy so far, much too easy perhaps. She was methodical; kept an address book.' He held up the little leather book that Elsa had always carried in her bag. And on one of the old snaps, in the familiar handwriting and the green ink, below his scribble saying *'Je voudrais bien vous dire'* (their codeword) — 'Martin darling, believe it or not, I cried.' The snap was of the two of them, sitting on the terrace of the Lido, drinking gin from the look of the glasses.

He felt rage. He had torn up what letters or snaps he still had, throwing them in the stove under Sophia's mocking, indifferent, secretly commanding eye. But this bitch could never bear to lose or leave anything. She probably had little wax dolls with pins stuck in them.

'Tell me now,' said Van der Valk, 'why were you in that street?'

He knew they would keep asking that. 'I don't know. I like the street. I like that part of the town. I don't know why. I've walked that way before sometimes.'

'But you didn't know she lived there?'

'No.' Did he? Had he? But he had not — he knew he had not been in the house.

Van der Valk was staring at him as though he could read him like print. 'I'll accept that, for the moment. Let's get back to the point. We're checking everybody in the address book, naturally. We'll check anybody else who isn't in and ought to be, maybe. These aren't business addresses. Somebody, could be man, could be woman, shot her and ran down those stairs into the street. Somebody youngish and active; ran down two at a time. That's clear from what Bouwman says. He's a trained observer and accustomed to being a witness; I've no reason to doubt him. You'll tell me he maybe made the whole thing up; shot her himself. Maybe he did. But it would have to make sense first. I saw him when he came in here, and after, in his own flat. I smoke too much, but I've a good sense of smell. He stank of his radio thing – all new and packed in smelly cardboard; plastic and tools; oil and dust and the sweets he was eating. He doesn't smoke either; one of these secret toffee fiends. Her room smelt strongly of cigarette smoke, of fumes from the gun, her very distinctive perfume, and I should say herself.'

Martin could not help shutting his eyes, remembering Elsa's smell.

'No,' went on the other slowly, 'I don't believe in Bouwman. Too like a story, too unreal. Men like that don't get involved with their neighbours. I don't wash him out but I need convincing. I attach a lot of importance to that smell. Bouwman hadn't washed or tidied himself; he was in a stew; he just came round here. It's not far. I had a good look at his hands.'

Van der Valk put his elbows on the table. 'Suppose you tell me when you saw her last.'

'I'd have to think.'

'Think then. We've plenty of time.'

Martin thought.

'In a flat on the Lauriersgracht. Would have been the first year I was married – five years ago anyway. A man lives – lived anyway – there, whom I know slightly, and he invited us for an evening – not formal you know, just a drink and conversation; I'd got friendly with him over a book he was illustrating. When we got there she was sitting drinking coffee and being charming. Man's name is Pieters and it's the Marnixstraat end more or less, on top of a café; I can't remember the number.'

'What sort of relationship was there between you then?'

'We had parted a year before, in bitterness and rage. I hated her because I was a little afraid of her. What her feelings were

I didn't know or care; she had seemed unable to accept the idea that my life no longer revolved round her.'

'What was it like there in this house?'

'Horrible. There wasn't a row or anything; nobody else noticed any tension and the evening would have been pleasant enough, I suppose. I felt that I couldn't handle the situation as competently as I wished – I wasn't sufficiently detached. It bothered me to see her; I was hostile and embarrassed and she was laying herself out to be winning. She was still a bit under my skin and I knew she felt that. Maybe she expected me to say, "Come on, let's go!" – she put enormous force into persuading me that nothing mattered but her. I don't doubt that when I didn't roll over with my paws in the air she went home in a black fury, ready to bite the carpet. She couldn't bear to lose anything. I had left her for a woman she despised and thought a trivial fancy of mine. When I married the woman she couldn't accept it. – What the hell am I telling you all this for?'

Van der Valk laughed, rubbing his nose.

'You're telling me because it relieves you and still pleases you to talk about her. You see that she's still important to you.'

Martin laughed too, unwillingly. 'Only because she's dead. And because you're digging at my emotions. I haven't thought about her more than casually above twice in the last five years – since that episode in fact. I never saw her again consciously.' Directly he spoke the word he knew Van der Valk had noticed it. But he made no comment; he was staring at the wall.

He seemed to make up his mind.

'I'm not charging you with this. Not yet anyway, and possibly not at all. It's like this. I can charge you formally with murder, because frankly I've enough to do so, and then the examining magistrate takes over the depositions and interrogations. You won't get out of it in a hurry then, even if you're as innocent as Joan of Arc. I'm holding you on a reasonable presumption that you are the probable author of a grave criminal action. Whether I believe that's immaterial. You could refuse to answer, demand a lawyer, hold out on me; in that event I'll charge you so quick you'll be on the magistrate's desk like a telegram. But I would prefer not to charge you, but hold you for a little, because I think you can tell me a great deal I want to know. Help me, and I might be in a position to release you in a week, instead of your riding the circuit on the parquet.

'On the other hand, suppose you're guilty. Likely there are all sorts of extenuating circumstances and hanky-panky. Once I charge you, you can get your lawyer and fight it out and refuse to answer me. So you've a choice. Tell me everything as freely as you did just now, as though I were one of those psychiatrist idiots, and I'll break this, and clear you in the process. Or clam up – I'll charge you today, it'll take six months to come to trial, and even if you get off half the country will still say a smart lawyer got you off. I've given you good advice; please yourself. Here, have a cigarette.'

'I don't want a cigarette,' said Martin crossly. He got up and looked out of the window, jingling the keys in his pockets. He knew he was being had, had the classic police way, *à la chansonette*. Lulled into a sense of security he would give himself away. Suppose he was schizophrenic – suppose he had really killed Elsa? They would have him anyway. A simple order would jump him straight into the examining magistrate's arms. He could just see that lipless, joyless, rimless-glasses smile they all had. He made his choice, and wondered whether it showed him sane or the contrary.

'I'll trust you; I'll go along with you on this.'

The other was staring again, tapping his pen on his teeth.

'Don't have any illusions. If this still points to you, not overwhelmingly but just whelmingly, I can still charge you. I throw the cards on the table and go where they point. Get it?'

'Yes.'

'Understood.' He spoke with genuine friendliness. 'You aren't getting sacrificed. I'll go a long way to break this one, with

22

newspapers buzzing round like wasps already. I'm a naughty policeman, you think. Threaten people, lead them on, trick them, beat them up sometimes. All just for credit with my boss, you think. Not quite. I want simply to understand this woman, because I have an impression that if I do I'll know why she was killed. I know why, I'll know who. That's all. Now I'll give you as much latitude as I can. Books, food, anything like that; you can see your wife every day if you like in someone's presence. Means the man on guard duty. And if I take you out, no policemen and no handcuffs; break from me and you're cooked, you know that.'

He threw the pen down; it rolled off the table on to the floor. *'Verdomme!'* he said, stooping. On cue, the phone rang. He straightened, red.

'Van der Valk. Yes. Good. A second . . . I'm listening, shoot.' There was a persistent quacking mumble. The pen travelled steadily over paper. 'All right, thanks. You'll have a transcript for me when you can? Thanks again. 'Bye.' He put the phone down, leaned back and studied his paper. 'Taking you into my confidence like this is against all standard police procedure. I might give you some information that helps you build a false picture. You risk my paying out a lot of line, and lassoing you at the end of it. Right? We're quits.'

'Don't talk so goddam much,' said Martin.

Van der Valk stuck a cigarette in his mouth, lit it and pointed with the burning match at Martin. 'Just before she was killed she'd made love. You see what that means. Some information and some interesting presumptions. A man killed her. A woman did not leave that evidence behind, not even one of these rubberglove queens in a white overall that play with bulls on breeding farms. A man killed her, very shortly after making love to her. And it was a man who knew her because it was her gun. Based on your knowledge of her, how does that fit in? Presumption one, was she a whore?'

Martin felt sick. The policeman's bad and crude joke had had the effect, probably intended, of detaching him from the unwilling tenderness he had still somehow felt for Elsa. He felt nothing now, except the wish to be sick. The voice pursued him down a tunnel of nausea.

'I should have explained,' it said quietly, reasonably. 'That was the medical report. Doctor did a quick check on the spot of course, but next day in detail. I should have had that yesterday but that I was running after you. She isn't a person any more, you know. An exercise, medico-legal; that's all.'

Martin thought hard, gripping words to stop being sick. 'No, she wasn't a whore – not when I knew her that is. Capable of it, yes. She had a good upbringing, but that doesn't stop anyone. Kept from it more out of economic reasons than by character.' 'What's important in her is gone,' he thought, 'and what I say will not affect her and cannot hurt her now. It is now without importance.'

'If she was a whore we'll soon find out,' said Van der Valk comfortably. 'These semipros who do it for fun aren't easy to keep a file on, you might say, but that call girl stuff is known to plenty of people. Probably find out easy in the Josef Israels. Presumption two, was she a nymphomaniac?'

'Yes. Not indiscriminate; she didn't go about seizing men and jumping into beds with them. Don't know if a type like that exists,' meditatively. 'Never met one myself.'

'Nor have I,' said Van der Valk pleasantly. 'Stop lingering over happy memories.'

'She couldn't live without men. I think she was a bit masochistic physically. She liked to be abused, sworn at, ordered round, punished, deprived for a day or two. She liked being beaten. That's physical. Mentally, she developed complete power over her men. Not only me; I saw it with other men. They no longer lived unless she was there breathing life into them. Like puppies, looking up with sad eyes for a pat. She made them do ridiculous things to satisfy her appetite for domination. I think she liked sex for that reason too; it didn't give her much pleasure, it was the feeling of mastery that was better, sucking all the guts out of a man. She was simply a

24

witch. She could take all a man's will and substitute her own, leaving him a zombie. She called him and he came; she wanted something done – the poor *sufferd* went and did it. He felt resentment, so he would drag her all limp and unresisting to a divan and thrash her; make him a man again for half an hour.'

Van der Valk was sitting upright, eyes wide, like a man whose team has just scored a brilliant goal.

'Lovely. What I've missed!' He brought his palm down on the table with a slap. 'Lunch-time, *jongen*. Canteen grub for you, but your wife can bring you things when she comes in. I'll give the guards all the necessary instructions about you; you won't have a bad life. No office to worry about. A holiday,' he added with facetious ferocity, 'more than I get. You can write a book about it maybe when it's all over. Come on. I've a few jobs, after eating; then, *jongen*, you and I are going to take a little ride.'

Van der Valk had the car ready; without speaking he threw it into gear and headed towards the town. It is not possible to avoid the mid-afternoon traffic in Amsterdam; progress is fitful. The lights on the Muntplein were against them; Martin stared at the bell tower and the corner of the Singel with a new eye. Being in the half-world of the police gave a new definition to people. All these people, staring at Vroom's window display by the antheap where the Kalverstraat begins; all those others heading with an alert, expectant look towards the other antheap of the Reguliersbreestraat, as though in the Rembrandtplein they would be given a lovely present; who were they? People with no idea in their head except business – for if the motto of Germany is *Befehl ist Befehl* (Orders are orders) that of Holland is quite surely *Zaken zijn zaken* (Business is business). And some innocent little pleasures too – coffee and a nice big creamy chunk of tart in Doelen or Polen. What about the people taking a quick connoisseur's sniff at the weather – cold now and lowering from a yellowish leaden sky?

Snow soon, doubtless, and ice perhaps, and the children asking for their skates. Were they thinking only of pea soup in ten thousand homes, and curly kale with boiled sausage in ten thousand more? Looking forward to the days soon when *Sinterklaas* would be coming with his *knecht,* and the bakers would all be displaying initials made of puff pastry stuffed with frangipane?

There were murderers among them, frauds, perverts, thieves, *souteneurs.* Psychopaths, many of them, no doubt: poor old men who followed little girls in parks. But many too were criminals, who enjoyed seducing virgins, who poisoned their wives, who would as soon steal from the poor as from the rich, especially as it was generally easier, who lived unworried and secure on the profits from the nasty little follies and meannesses of all the mass. Parasites, gamblers, pornographers. Victims. Van der Valk's professional eye was upon them too. Was Elsa's murderer here as well, more concerned at the moment with the traffic policeman in his little steel tower than with the featureless *rechercheur* in the featureless little Volkswagen?

Van der Valk turned right past the Hôtel de l'Europe, wound round and into the courtyard of the Binnen Gasthuis, the big hospital that is the outpost of Amsterdam's last old quarter. Martin always felt pleasure here in these narrow old streets alongside the canals, which have not yet been all filled in or chewed away by the ceaseless friction and vibration of traffic. They walked quickly down the cool antiseptic corridor. Van der Valk seemed to know his way; his soles tapped round corners, taking bearings without hesitating. Martin knew now what was on hand and breathed deeply, filling his lungs as full as he could of an air already corrupted. He was not going to let them make a fool of him, leading him by the nose to a surprise that was perhaps supposed to make him give at the knees. He strode like a free man, and gripped himself firmly in front of the ghastly door marked 'Department of Pathology'.

There was a warm cheerful little office, with a pretty young

26

woman drinking tea, an impassive woman typing, with too much experience in her quiet, kind old face, and a lean, dark young man in an overall, standing in front of an open filing cabinet with a bunch of cards in his hand. A faint disgusting reek – was that formaldehyde he wondered? – possessed every heart in the little office. The young woman looked up. Her smooth blonde hair lay high and sculptured above a forehead like a pearl. Her smile was fresh and untouched by formaldehyde or the terrible filing cards. Her teeth were too large. Van der Valk spoke in the important low chatter of someone with an unimportant errand.

'Oh yes,' she said. She had a gentle, hoarse voice. She gave a semicircular, meditative look; nobody paid the least heed. She got up, showing a fragile figure, legs a tiny bit too thin, hands and feet a tiny bit too big. She flipped her starched white skirt into place with an automatic, unselfconscious gesture.

'The head of the department is out,' nodding towards an inner office with a curt plastic plate on the forbidding panel. 'I know about the business more or less. Will you come please?'

A corridor, full of doors. Two or three obvious laboratory technicians glancing incuriously as they went on accustomed, undramatic errands. The smell of formaldehyde was stronger. Another door, swinging on bronze hinges with an effortless, noiseless lunge like a huge mouth opening.

A hum of refrigerating machinery. Light flicked on from daylight neons, incandescent and chilly on the opal tiles. The pretty girl walked to an office table and flipped a pop-up file like those for telephone numbers. Find-it-quick, thought Martin. She looked in a day-book then, biting her thumb absently. With a nod she walked quickly towards the wall of countersunk filing cabinets and slid one out, seven feet of corpse-container, unconcerned as a croupier when the player says 'a card'. Martin stood by her, smelling the faint kind scent of her hair.

The face was not shrunken, nor yellow, nor horrible. It was absolutely neutral. There was no look of peace nor faint smile nor any cliché at all. Dead bodies are not frightening, nor are they communicative. There is simply nothing there. The hair, blonde still but greyer than he remembered it, lay in soft waves behind the rather heavier jaw. He glanced at Van der Valk, who was studying the face as though he expected to see a name written there; at the girl who stood quietly looking at nothing, her hands in her overall pockets. Martin stared slowly at the naked body, neat and soldierly. The breasts were still firm; the stomach, punctuated by four little dark marks in an irregular quadrangle, was not much wrinkled. The remembered deep, gay hollow under the hipbone was unchanged. The face was still beautiful, the coarse skin set in remarkably firm contours over the high intelligent bones. Elsa had always looked her best by artificial light. Martin felt a last glimmer of tenderness move in him.

'Did she take long to die?'

'Don't ask me, I wasn't there,' said Van der Valk with his brutal joviality.

The girl answered detachedly, looking at neither of them. 'Not so very long. Time enough to have brought her back, perhaps, if they'd found her at once. Pretty dim perhaps, with four bullets, but possible. But she didn't have very much pain, probably. She would guess she was going to die.' With no emotion she made a sign of the cross. 'Ready?'

The little glimmer of tenderness vanished as the file sighed home. Finally, Elsa was gone. Martin felt no more emotion than the girl. Van der Valk put a cigarette in his mouth, and took it out again. He looked at Martin with little wrinkles of gaiety in his eyelids.

'Wait for me in the car. I won't be five minutes.' As Martin left he heard, 'How long for a full path. breakdown? Everything on the book.'

Outside, Martin lit a cigarette with a deep breath of relief. Van der Valk drove back to the bureau without a word. When he was pleasantly settled again at his table he put his elbows on it and rubbed his nose thoughtfully. Then he got up and went to a steel cabinet, dragged open a drawer and came out with a brown paper parcel. He undid the string leisurely.

'This is what she was wearing. It tells me nothing. I can have it sent to the chemist's, but I've a very strong opinion that it would be a waste of time. This is not to my mind a question for someone looking at dust with a microscope; it is more psychological. Smell these clothes; they smell of her. That jade signet ring was on her hand. Always was, wasn't it? The gold is very worn, and has been mended, maybe more than once. There's nothing missing that I would have expected to find. Admitted, so far I've only been over everything superficially. Tomorrow, *jongen*, you and I are going to walk as far as the Josef Israels; reconstruct the crime maybe. You,' he guffawed, 'can hold the gun. No use shooting me, I'm insured. Right now ...' He was handling the clothes like a textile buyer, pawing them, thought Martin, as though there were still a woman in them. He felt the texture, holding everything to the light. He threw them aside contemptuously. 'It's nothing. Tells me nothing I didn't know.'

Martin watched him sullenly, sour disgust sitting on his face, deliberately obvious. The man was playing with Elsa's shoe like a bloody pervert; did he get some obscure pleasure out of fiddling with these rags? His eyes rested on Martin and became absent.

'The anatomy lesson of Dr Tulp. How did you like Dr Tulp? Nice looking, isn't she? Bit thin, but better looking than your girl-friend. We're going to have a little lesson now, on your anatomy instead of hers. Pity I couldn't bring Dr Tulp with me; she might have livened you up.'

Martin snarled like a teased leopard. 'You've got one dead whore; want another one live? Stop making one out of me then; quit this mucking about, taking me to places where I'm expected to scream and faint or something. What do you expect to get out of breaking it off in me? Start me sobbing, and saying, "Oh please, please; I'll tell you all"? I know what she smelt like; you don't have to shove her underclothes in my face.'

Van der Valk was laughing heartily.

'So I looked at that bloody woman doctor in the hospital. That doesn't mean I wanted to take her to bed.'

'Why not? I did,' said Van der Valk equably with his damned confident, cagy, sympathetic grin. 'You're coming on, learning now. Did you think it was all guaranteed painless? No anaesthetics in the police department, *jongen*. No nice nurse to comb your hair. I've got to take your skin off, and the quickest way; I've got to find out what you know. You know too much about this business. Some of it maybe you don't know you know; I'll have it just the same. You really think you're not involved? "All right," you think, "so I was outside the house; that doesn't put me inside, that doesn't put the gun in my hand." You believe me; you're in deep.'

'*Klets*,' said Martin, 'that's all bluff. Why the hell am I in deep? You can't get any judge or any court to say I killed her just because I knew her once and I was outside her door. You can hold me here for ever, but you aren't getting me to say I killed her when I didn't. Not even by beating me up. Are you going to beat me up?'

'I'm going to let you beat yourself up, *jongen*,' said Van der Valk sunnily. 'Nobody's talking about courts and judges, though you might be surprised to know what they could make you say. I'm just demonstrating what would be obvious to anyone with any sense. You've brains enough but you've no *nous*. You're involved with a woman. That woman is dead. She was killed. Someone killed her. Now I'm not giving you this crap about society, and the protection of it and the duties owed to it and so on – that's all baby talk for the electorate. This is a plain thing. Some actions are simply wrong, morally. Death by violence is a grave wrong, the more so because you destroy something that cannot be replaced or rebuilt. You can't detach yourself from that as a whole, in general. But here, in particular, even less. You – you're part of this crime.

30

You loved her, lived with her and were part of her. You're involved and I don't care whether you were outside the door or in a café in Purmerend. If you killed her I'll find out – you'll tell me. You're going to start right now by telling me what you were really doing in the street, and don't begin that pretty fairy story either about admiring the pretty moon like a pretty cheese in the pretty canal.'

Martin gave an unwilling grin.

'You're making me feel guilty, a fool and a bastard.'

'Ha!' shouted Van der Valk happily, 'for all I know you're all three. You knew she lived there, didn't you?'

'I must have been told, I suppose, some time. But I didn't realize . . .'

'You didn't realize. It wasn't real. You just went there with a vague idea, hoping to sort of accidentally run across her. You would rather have liked to be in a position to hurt her – Don't interrupt. Look, this is the way it happened. Doesn't bear any sign at all of a perverted, psychopath murder. Someone – I neither say nor have any firm idea it was you – got into a sudden blind rage, saw red with anger, jealousy, pain, humiliation – call it what you like. Could have been you; fits, or could be made to fit. Gun looks like premeditation, but I don't see it that way. I prefer to think that at some time a man had been playing with that gun, as a toy, and had slipped it in his pocket, make him feel tough. Then he got a sudden onrush of sheer, vicious rage, and suddenly the gun was in his hand. He'll try temporary insanity when I get him.'

Van der Valk was studying him carefully through a fan of smoke. 'Won't wash. A woman throws you off course, maybe, puts you in the wrong gear, races your motor. Doesn't make you mad. Then everyone in the world's mad. Jesus, what a speech! You stew on that; I'm up to here. Go on, buzz off and tell them to lock you up. Simmer quietly and in the morning cough it all up; I'll be there with a basin.'

Martin felt tired; so tired that he could scarcely stand on his legs. He stood feeling nothing but exhaustion and a sort of dull ache. He walked through the still guardroom and into his open cell, collapsed on the mattress and fell instantly asleep.

When he woke, an hour or two later, it was still quiet, and quite dark; he lit a cigarette and lay thinking, not getting anywhere with it; his ideas were vague and shapeless. He saw at some moment the guard in the doorway, with the pipe in his teeth.

'Come on and eat – don't let the coffee get cold. Sour herring tonight. While you eat you can talk to your wife – she's out here waiting for you.'

Martin jumped off the bed with vivacity.

In the shabby guardroom Sophia looked like a bird of paradise. Her perfume gave life to the stale air; her smile illuminated the world of policemen. She pushed a parcel forward on the table.

'What's in it?' he asked, like a child.

'Smoked eel, cigars, the French history book, *Chance,* and a big bar of chocolate.' She smiled as one does to a child. He kissed her with absorption and lit a cigar with pleasure; the coffee in the big enamel mug was hot and surprisingly good. Sophia watched him with love, sitting elegantly on the corner of the table. The guard took his pipe out of his teeth, brought a chair forward and was buried deeply, instantly, in a fearful book with vampires on the cover.

Sophia crossed her knees and said, 'Give me a cigarette then.' She screwed her eyes against the smoke and asked abruptly: 'Did you kill her?'

'Ah, darling. Leave it a while. I've had Van der Valk being clever with it all day. Of course I didn't kill her. They're hanging on to me simply because I knew her. She's dead now; you ought to be glad.'

'You're talking like a child and a fool. "Ought to be glad!" – aren't you ashamed of yourself? Van der Valk will take you to the cleaners if you persist in being so stupid. I've seen him; he told me straightforwardly that he, personally, emphasized, did not believe you'd killed her. I'm by no means so sure. How often had you been to the Josef Israels when you were supposed to be working on some scheme in Amsterdam?'

'You aren't still jealous? The woman's dead and I know nothing about it. How many men wasn't she involved with, for Christ's sake?'

'I'm jealous of her dead and alive where you're concerned.' She threw her cigarette in a fast sparkling arc into the coke bucket.

'I never saw her; I never went in the house; I never spoke to her.'

'Yes, I know you're telling yourself that, but are you quite certain? Did that witch throw a spell on you again? I can't bear it if you won't tell me the truth. You were mooning still after her and she's been killed. Killed. To Mr Van der Valk that's just a job, and to you perhaps it's a great relief; maybe you've dodged a responsibility. You had one to her, I think. I don't remind you of your responsibilities to me, to your home. Certainly I hated the woman, but she was shot in the belly and crawled over the floor bleeding inside and then she lay and died, while you were taking a nice walk in the street. My husband, sitting in prison. No, I don't believe you killed her. If you had I'd wait twenty years outside a prison for you. But I think you're hiding part of the truth. You tell me, you hear? Not now; I can't stand here watching you trying to hold firm and deny it. I'll come back tomorrow.'

The policeman raised quiet china-blue eyes from his vampires. 'Goodnight, Mevrouw. Here, let me open the door for you. Happy to see you. Till tomorrow.'

Martin felt as if he had been struck by lightning. He made two big careful sandwiches, one with herring and the other with chocolate, took the French history, and said to the guard in as acid a voice as he could manage, 'Be a friend and lock me in. The next visitor will probably be the Minister for Social Affairs, worried about my morals.'

'Sleep well,' said the policeman without irony. The door shut with a clank; the keys fell on the floor and the guard cursed, mildly and unemotionally.

Van der Valk's pocket was full of keys; he fiddled and muttered before finding the right one. The flat in the house on the Josef Israelskade smelt stuffy and dusty, and was cold. The policeman put a match to the stove like a housewife.

'Crafty, see. I was here last night in my overcoat, stiff as an old plank. Stove had been cleaned out; damned policemen thinking they're going to find bones or buttons or something. All I had to do was lay it.'

Smoke curled aromatic at the top as it started to draw. Van der Valk looked triumphant as though he had done something extremely clever. Martin could see that he had gone solemnly round with the dustpan and the vacuum cleaner. 'Only a Dutch policeman would have done that,' he thought, amused. 'At home he probably has to take his shoes off before his wife allows him in the living-room.' The room was comfortable now, welcoming, and rapidly growing warmer.

The furniture was not new but there were some fairish pieces, mended possibly, but in good condition and of good period, simple and well-shaped. Some might have cost a lot. He had always admired Elsa's distinctive taste in the things she had around her. Van der Valk was busy puttering in the kitchen; Martin put more coke on the stove and shut the damper half way. Most of these houses had central heating now; he supposed most of this district had been built with oil-burners installed, but he preferred a stove; it was nicer because you could fiddle with it. Your fire; something personal to you. He started to wander round with his hands in his pockets. There was the writing desk that had helped to drag him into this. It told him nothing; was locked. The floor was covered with worn Persian rugs over cord carpet, and his eye told him they were good ones; auctions, he guessed. The pictures interested him. No banal chromolithographs here. Two nice prints from Guardi and a comic Longhi of a horrid old marquis in a beast-mask, dancing with a young fresh marquise in a loup. ('Hm,' thought Martin.) A well-known Mantegna excellently reproduced, in a very good gilt frame. And a handsome, heavy Flemish burgher's wife, peeling carrots in the seventeenth century, rather damaged, cleaned but seemingly not restored, very well painted. Original, he guessed, but no terribly great sale-room value because not clearly attributed. On the coffee table was a Lalique bird that he had given her, which he recognized with a tiny start. Everything was well polished and well looked after. The curtains were a good brocade, with a bird-and-foliage motif, faded to autumn tints; bronze and burnt orange, *feuille morte* and olive green. Several shelves of books, including a few that were his, and a good number more that he remembered, all rather heavy with art. Balinese art, Chinese art, Hindu art, Italian majolica, German baroque, marks on pottery and porcelain, English Georgian silver, Sèvres in the time of Louis XV. He did not greatly care for Elsa's art, but the figurines she designed were gay and fresh, and sometimes original and delightful, in spite of most being tourist: Volendamse fishermen and farmer's wives from Brabant.

She must have made a bit of money from them, he thought; some had been reproduced in their thousands, and sold enormously at home as well as to tourists.

Van der Valk came in with a tray, coffee-pot balanced carefully, proud as a girl a week married. Martin grinned at his careful, pleased face above Elsa's china. Modern, he noticed, a well-known design by Rosenthal.

'I'll be Mum,' he said, and poured the coffee with enjoyment.

'No biscuits,' said the policeman in a regretful voice.

'What happens to all these things now?'

'There isn't any will or anything,' making himself comfortable. 'She was a great one for hiding things, but no secrets or incriminating documents turned up, not even a nice blackmailing letter. Her next of kin's automatically her husband; they weren't divorced or anything. He can do as he likes with all this eventually. Examining magistrate decides when it isn't necessary any more. You know, mysterious scratches on the lavatory door, might be a clue to something. They never are, but policemen don't ever believe that.'

Martin thought of Erich van Kampen, thin and nervous as a flamingo, his coffee-cup rattling in the saucer. The man had asked nothing except to be left in peace; if he had had a quiet, peaceful, placid wife he would not have drunk so much.

'Where is the husband now?'

'In The Hague. He's some sort of fairly important *fonctionnaire*, in a Department of State Archives of some sort; I'm none too clear.'

'Yes, he used to be an authority on documents, authenticating them and deciphering them and so forth. He had some university job here, I recall. And what about him?'

'Nothing about him. Got a mistress of twenty-two, very nice girl, all luscious and cushiony, and he's only terrified that somebody might make a scandal for him in The Hague. I was there last night. He made sad faces and wound his hair round his fingers, but he's absolutely wrapped up in his girl, quite self-centred you see, and he's practically forgotten what his wife's name was. Have to look a bit nearer home if you want a handy whipping-boy; Tuesday night he was at the Kurhaus in Scheveningen and about twenty people saw him there. That's what is on my plate, to discover and check all the people whom she knew, who were even faintly familiar in this house – I mean that they knew where the lavatory was without asking, and helped wash glasses. The moths around the candle flame. See what account they give of themselves, especially for Tuesday night; bloody stupid job because they'll half of them have forgotten and the other half can't be substantiated. Point is to find whether they had a psychological likelihood as types in her life. Pity we've no more information about the physical possibility. You were there outside, you ought really to have seen or heard someone. The door slam, for instance. Think back.'

'No, and that's funny too. The way Bouwman told it there was a slam, and someone running. But I heard nothing.'

'And saw nobody?'

'No; but I didn't even see the policeman, so I wasn't in a seeing mood. If you told me a tank went by full of Cubans with beards I wouldn't be able to call you a liar.'

'I wish sometimes,' with deep feeling, 'that a tank full of Cubans with beards would arrive at the Palais de Justice. If you knew about the persecution I'm putting up with from the examining magistrate on your account ... Never mind that now. Just put yourself back to when you lived with her. First of all, where? The address I mean.'

'Here in Amsterdam. Matthew Marisstraat. Number eighty-seven.'

'And she lived there with her husband?'

'Yes, it was his flat.'

'He found out?'

'He knew; must have known as well as you can without actually catching people in bed together. But he refused to see or admit or talk about it. He just wouldn't accept it. Always friendly to me, never constrained or false, talked about anything, asked my advice sometimes, gave his own at others; treated me as a close family friend. He could even be personal – "Don't you think Elsa's got rather thinner?" – "Don't you think she ought to take cod-liver oil?" – that sort of remark. He was always affectionate with her in public. They had appalling rows fairly frequently; she always claimed that he began them when drunk, that he was jealous and possessive. I felt afterwards that she deliberately encouraged those rows. She loved nothing better than a good row. So he was possessive – what man isn't, with his own wife?'

'Did he have anything to do with your split?'

'No. She wanted to make out that he was attacking her, to enlist my loyalty further, but he never said a word. I realize that I'm whitewashing him. He had his dirty tricks, but even those she could turn to her advantage. When he was out

37

having a few drinks she stayed at home all right, but she didn't sit all pathetic knitting. No, the split was entirely between herself and me.'

'Over another man?'

'Over another woman. She accused me of sleeping with her out of habit and running after another woman in between — "making a fool of myself with a silly little girl". The silly little girl is now my wife. It was all quite true of course, but left out that she was doing exactly the same. She had another man. She had two.'

'Lovely. Go on.'

'There was some German, from the factory which makes a lot of her figures. Big man, not fat, you know, but mighty well filled out. Very amusing; wonderful company. Can't think of the name; heard it of course but don't recall. And there was Herman. Whom I know, very slightly. His name's Ketelboer. His friends call him Kalkoen, don't ask me why. Lives in a houseboat over somewhere by the Bilderdijkkade. Big boat, a good twenty-five metres long. All Japanese inside. I've been there, but only at night, about twice, once with her I think.

'He fascinated her. Svengali stuff. He's a doctor, good one too, I believe. Does things for your muscles, treats all sorts of obscure nervous conditions, some sort of osteopath. Bit on the line of that blind woman who does dancers. Plays the piano very well. Plenty of screws loose; goes in for obscure composers, knows the whole of Frescobaldi and Scriabin by heart. She was always running to him, after he said clever things about her hands. Did you notice her hands?'

'That she bit her nails.'

'Yes, but as well as that she had rather ugly clever hands; when she held them straight the fingers bent right up backwards. They curved towards one another too. Thumbs were funny as well; oddly articulated. Think now they were greedy hands. But clever. Herman got excited, told her she was a natural sculptor. Made her do hand exercises, and started off the figurine business. All those farmers. You know that shop

38

on the corner of the Spuistraat? – everywhere, come to that. *Objets d'art,* like the Copenhagen goosegirls but better, not so slick and much better visualized. Typical Dutch, for types that despise wooden shoes and miniature windmills. All the high-class souvenir shops sell buckets of them. She made a good enough thing out of it, seemingly; I mean this flat's not bad.'

'Yes, there's a studio in the spare room. We'll look in a minute. Tell me first who else she knew. Men.'

'She didn't know many women. Very few women friends, and those a lot younger than she was. Women her own age mostly hated her. There was a man who worked for the Vara radio company in Hilversum. Had something special about his voice. Arie ... *Dingus dingus,* something like Heemstede – you know, when you hear it you always say "Of course, I won't forget another time," but you always do. There was Toon Sietsema the cartoonist. Don't honestly think she saw an awful lot of him after he married. Henry Ruysbroeck, writes the column, big man with a Roman nose. You see the sort of thing. All interesting, all artists a bit, all a bit daft. But she knew many people whom I hardly knew at all – vague names but no face, vague face and no name; came occasionally and wrote lots of letters.'

'Just habitués of the house, at present. What about her family?'

'There's a Papa de Charmoy, lives in Brussels, must be pretty old; horrible old man, always marrying his secretaries. Import-export with Brazil, I believe. There's a sister somewhere in Germany. There's a cousin in Amersfoort who owns a garage, very rich and didn't care for her much, and there's a brother who lived in Algiers when I knew her. There was a sister married to a diplomatist in Mexico, but she died. She didn't see any of her family much. All big letter-writers though.'

The way Van der Valk grinned Martin thought, 'That's no news to you; you've had a good go at the writing desk.'

'That's a good start,' said the policeman, 'gives me a fair idea of what I'm up against. Some of these people will have lost touch, others will be able to give further names, more information. Out of these little scraps I should be able to form a clearish picture of who she saw, and where. Gradually we will have her whole up-to-date circle of close acquaintances, and we've only to hold them upside down and shake a bit and a murderer will pop out. Simple enough, but taking time and a hell of a boring slog through oceans of irrelevance. Just the opposite to all the books, where everything is complicated as a government loan and is all done in one evening by a genius sitting down. Pour some more coffee out. Don't you think I make good coffee?'

'Not bad,' said Martin seriously.

Van der Valk drank the coffee at a gulp. He walked back into the little passage that linked the front door with the other rooms, saying 'Come on.'

He was thinking aloud after his habit, standing in the kitchen doorway.

'Small flat admitted, but she did it single-handed; kept it pretty clean too. She had a washing machine, did her own cooking, cleaning; seems to have liked housekeeping; unusual in a way in that type of woman. There's a box full of sewing and there's half a sweater on knitting needles.'

'She liked to cook, and she liked sewing,' Martin answered absently, from the bedroom. 'She was a pretty good cook too; liked food.'

The bedroom was like the living-room, with good and well-shaped furniture, heavy and well-made in a pale bright wood, inlaid with marquetry in some darker wood. Friesian perhaps, thought Martin; she had Friesian blood on the mother's side. A big double bed, so broad as to be almost square; a gigantic wardrobe, and a dressing table with three good glasses, old, faded glasses that reflected with the soft sheen of age. It was all far too big for the flimsy modern house with its small rooms, but it had beauty, and dignity. Deceptive, he thought;

not really what you'd expect of a whore's bedroom. The bed was stripped.

'Police chemist probably enjoying himself with the sheets,' said Van der Valk, making one of his horrible jokes.

There was a hand-made Smyrna rug on the polished floor. Police fingers had tidied here too; 'carefully folding up cami-knickers,' thought Martin happily, 'running a careful arm inside nylons to see if they were snagged; using a meticulous clothes-brush, and twisting loose blonde hairs neatly into a Kleenex, that could be crumpled and thrown in the basket with the other tissues stained with make-up.'

'Have you been through everything?' he asked.

'No, haven't had time. Shan't either, unless I find it worth the trouble. You were right enough about one thing that you told me; I turned this up.' He rummaged among old shoe-boxes and bundled-up blouses, old scarves and odd gloves that cluttered the top shelf of the wardrobe. 'Pah, it would hurt, that. And she got fun out of it. I'd have given her a few real ones if I'd known the trouble she had cooked up for me.' He had a little riding switch in his hand, flicking it with a supple nasty noise in the still room. It was only a leather thong plaited round a core. Martin handled it a moment with a sour smile under sardonic eyes.

'Seems the same. I've no particular reason to recognize it.' He tossed it back, bored. 'Things lose all importance once the owner's dead. You look at Napoleon's little hat in a museum and you couldn't care less.'

'Good,' said the other appreciatively. 'Hate myself having to fiddle with dead junk. This now; I'd throw it in the dust-bin. Still, maybe the examining magistrate has a daughter who takes riding lessons.' He threw it on the shelf. 'Studio's next door.'

It was an ordinary room, bigger than the bedroom, had probably been designed as a bedroom but used for work be-cause the light was good. One wall was all shelves full of rub-bish: paperbacks, magazines, scraps of odd materials; lumps of sculptor's clay long gone hard; a few of the unglazed originals of Elsa's figurines; some practice models or failed efforts, abandoned half finished; two or three head-and-shoulder busts that seemed portraits, not very successful.

'See anybody you know?' asked Van der Valk, grinning.

'No,' he answered, not very interested. A large ashtray still half full of cigarette ends; a few reference books; an expensive illustrated *History of Costume* and *Traditional Peasant Costumes of Europe*.

The room was neither as tidy nor as clean as the others. There were two portable paraffin stoves. A large portfolio was full of pencil sketches and some elaborate water-colours of the figures as visualized. A wooden cigar-box held tools for working details of the clay, most no more than strips or wires that had been hammered or twisted the way she wished. A few were surgeon's tools; one was a sardine-tin opener. There was no furniture to speak of; a wooden articulated figure lay on a sagging couch, and there was a wooden kitchen table with an old chair tucked under it. A smeary cotton overall hung on a nail driven into the door. Two photographic arc-lamps had their flexes looped carelessly round them in a corner; a few gay posters were pinned to the bare walls; and an old sheepskin rug emphasized worn lino. The windows had plain cotton curtains. Martin stared around with rather faint interest.

'Did you have everything finger-printed?' with childish curiosity.

'Oh, God yes,' groaned Van der Valk. 'Waste of time. Nothing to go on and not much of that. Keep them just in case but I hate all that piddling about. If it isn't done there's a row, and it reassures the bloody newspapers that the police are up to all the latest scientific discoveries. Seen them?'

'Yes,' said Martin with contempt. 'Calling her "a woman of a certain reputation" and "of questionable character!" Childish stupidity.'

'Ach, they haven't had any fun since Blonde Dolly was

knocked off over on the Achterburgwal,' said Van der Valk tolerantly. 'They dream of Rosemarie.'

The kitchen, thought Martin, was more interesting than the studio. As the policeman had noticed, Elsa had been a good housewife. Even when poor her food had been good. This kitchen woke more memories of her than the bedroom did, oddly. Next door was the douche and lavatory.

'I did print here with more enthusiasm,' said the voice behind him. 'Not cleaned so often, and a good surface. Got a man's here. See tomorrow if they're yours,' he added nastily. 'Papers are calling you the mysterious figure of the *demi-monde*. One thinks you might be her *souteneur*. They've had to make up a good deal. Luckily Bouwman is by nature and because of his job very discreet. He was wonderful with them, wouldn't tell anything; stiff as a mast and very much on his dignity. "I knew nothing of her life since I had no acquaintance with the unfortunate lady," he said. They're breathing down my neck, hoping to see the cat come out of the tree. Examining magistrate won't help them; I'll have to have something to give him today.'

He opened one of the little doors and brought out a bottle of gin; he leered, all sinister like a marijuana pusher. 'Police perks. If a reporter could see me now. Or the magistrate, screw him!'

He took two glasses and led the way back into the living-room, warm now and pleasant. Martin stared absently out of the window. The quay was almost deserted; a traveller – or could it be a reporter? – in a grey Opel was busily writing something into a green cardboard file balanced on his brief-case. A baker, pedalling his tricycle and singing happily with a cigar in his mouth; a prim housewife with a bulging shopping-bag, vulgar-looking red cabbage balanced on top. Clink went the gin-bottle on the lip of the glass behind him.

'You like sugar in your gin?' said the voice, pleased as a schoolboy with a stolen apple.

'No.'

Van der Valk's eyes were bright, as though he had had two or three already. He had his confidential, sympathetic look. *La chansonette*. 'I haven't taken my eyes off you since we came in, and you've given yourself away as clearly as though I'd been there myself when you were in this flat last.'

'Why don't you tell me what happened there then?'

'Your own voice trying to be funny sounds scared. When you came in, you weren't looking at a flat for the first time. Someone who does that looks all round; you looked at one point, at the writing desk, as though to check that nothing had been moved. The bedroom; anyone would expect it to be the big middle room where the studio is; that end room was designed for children. You knew the bedroom was at the end; while I was gabbling about the kitchen you walked straight to it, like a sleepwalker. So don't give me the witty stuff.'

'I've never been in the house before,' said Martin crossly. 'You're so goddam bright you imagine things.'

'Look, *jongen*, I know what you're scared of. You're scared your wife will know, and that's bloody silly, you know. The examining magistrate is yapping for your blood right now; he'll drill it out of you if that's what you want, and it can come out verbatim at the trial. Your wife will read it all in the papers if she isn't actually sitting there listening. You think that would be nicer for her? Tell now, and its importance comes to an end.'

'There's nothing to tell, can't you realize that?'

Van der Valk sipped his gin, and went on as though talking to himself. '*Jongen*, you've got to do it. There's been enough lying. The nasty thing, the thing I don't like about any police work, is the way everyone lies. All of a sudden there's a spotlight on them; they twist around like fish trying to dodge. It's no good; when you sit in my chair you can smell them lying. Take you; I knew you had something to hide from the moment you came into the Smedestraat. If I hadn't I'd be no good at my job.'

44

He finished his gin and licked round the edge of the glass, meditating.

'Little tiny lies. Men who tell their wives they earn a hundred and fifty a week when they touch two hundred; wives who tell their men the shoes cost twenty-five in a sale when they were forty-two fifty. Sons who tell their mas they were at Sunday-school; daughters who've been to the pictures with a girl friend. The one's snatched a handbag from an old woman and the other is carrying dirty pictures in her pocket which a man showed her in a bar. Once one of them sits there in your stool the lying starts in earnest. To whitewash themselves. The mothers will lie to whitewash the whole family.

'I expect it; I sit waiting for a moment to tell them what fools they're making themselves. Lying is never courage, or self-sacrifice; it's nothing but cowardice and self-deception all the way. You're hiding something from your wife rather than from me; have the guts to come out with it, and take a weight off her mind. As for me, I'm conducting a murder investigation. I've now no further time for liars. Especially the worst kind, and that's you. The kind that lie to dramatize themselves. Now, when were you in this house?'

Martin drank his gin at a gulp, shuddered violently, and slapped the glass down.

'Six weeks ago, pretty nearly.'

Van der Valk said 'Awk' like a man who has been shot, caught himself and said hospitably, 'I knew you had some brains left somewhere. Here, have some more gin.'

'All right; good lecture, fine climax. I couldn't stop myself; right from that first moment in the Smedestraat I was in a tangle and after that I was stuck with it. Directly you mentioned the Josef Israels I lied automatically.'

Van der Valk had his scribbling pad out on his briefcase; 'like the geyser in the Opel,' thought Martin.

'My wife knew I was lying too; women have an instinct for lies from their men. But one of the reasons why I find it dfficult to come out with it is that it's a damned ridiculous story. It's funny perhaps, but not easy to believe.'

'They never are,' said Van der Valk pleasantly. 'It's the lies that are so logical and reasonable.'

'It was in Herman's boat. I had got a ghastly thing in my back, about six weeks back as I told you. All of a sudden I couldn't straighten up; I was walking bent right over, like Groucho Marx. I went to a doctor, just shrugged his shoulders. Stay in bed, he said; nothing to be done except rest and warmth.

'I was fed up; busy at the time with a scheme, and there I was, locked solid and in a good deal of pain. I thought of Herman. He's a clever chap, rather nice too in his way. Anyway, I got into the bus; job it was; I couldn't sit in the car, the driving angle was wrong for me. I found Herman with a good deal of trouble, not knowing exactly where it was; he laughed like a fool at me, but he fixed me up and hardly hurt me at all; he has a way with massage.

' "All right," he said, "just rest there quietly for a little." I was all right, but I hardly dared move for a minute – you understand. Anyway, the door opened and there was Elsa. It was evening; I'd gone about five hoping to catch him with nobody there, since he sees people by appointment, you understand, just like any doctor. When I saw her I thought "Hell, this is going to be difficult," but she was at her best, very gay and full of nonsense, and it was like a party straight off. Herman is a witty bastard, and we were all laughing like a lot of kids. I can't convey the atmosphere.

'It seemed she'd done a figure; one of her farmers' girls, and it came out looking exactly like Queen Victoria. She was extremely funny about this beastly doll, and we were all thinking up one or another ridiculous obscenity. There was a feeling of friendship. We all ate together, I recall; I felt fine. I even remember Herman had raw *schinken* with kümmel in it, and a bottle of Picon. I'd had a gloomy day and been in some pain and a good deal of discomfort. Very slow and awkward, like

46

an old cow. You know, the feeling of high spirits at being suddenly free, and then a gay, funny time.

'*Enfin*, I had to go over to the Nassaukade to catch my bus back to Haarlem. Elsa said she'd drive me over, as it was on her way. She had an old car, battered Citroen. "Hell," she said, "messing with the bus, why don't I simply drive you as far as the Amsterdamse Buurt and you can get an ordinary Haarlem bus home? Tell you what; pass by my flat and I'll show you the princess – you've never been there have you? – and we'll go out through Amstelveen."

'Now understand me, I didn't want to refuse; I was a bit mortified at her being so nice. Even then it didn't properly strike me that I'd be a godawful fool to go in her flat. I made a few excuses, rather half hearted; I really wanted to go with her of course. "Ah, you may as well," she said, very uncon-cerned, "I've still got a couple of Mauriac books of yours, and if you don't take them you'll never get them back." I agreed. Call me a bastard if you like, but there were no real stupidities in my mind, more relief than anything else. I'd met a woman I'd always rather dreaded meeting, knowing it was likely some day, and there was no emotion, just an easy, friendly evening.

'She drove me over here; I sat there where you are. She had some apricot brandy, and showed me the Queen. It was funny too, extremely like, and had that look of stinking fish under the nose that really made it a good joke. And then hup! – while I was sitting there like the fool she must have thought me – she was sitting in my lap with her tongue burning my mouth. And, as of course she had planned, I was wanting her like fury. It was then the ridiculous part happened.

'She undressed in the lamplight, all luscious like a Titian, and I told her to get into bed. My back was tender, see, and I dndn't feel up to chasing round the furniture; I wanted her in comfort. Off she went like a lamb to the bedroom, climbed into bed, and I climbed in with her. And then believe me or not as you please, I couldn't lay a finger on her. I simply had no wish to touch her or kiss her or take her at all. Not

47

only indifference, but a sort of impatient dislike, as though stuck in a corner and unable to get away from somebody very boring and tiresome, when it's all you can do to stay polite.

'I was pretty shaken for a second. She was encouraging me and begging me all she knew, and I was like a frozen custard. I tried to pass it off, say my back was too painful and blah blah. She wasn't deceived, knew me too well for that. I've made love to her before, ill or not. She was furious – not really shrill but she lost her temper and stood there naked cursing at me, and threw a hairbrush.

'The cursing and the hairbrush made her simply funny; I wasn't shaken any more, just saw it all as rather ludicrous, was almost tempted to believe I'd done it on purpose to make a fool of her. You said that I was looking for an opportunity for getting back at her; I got it then. I told her what she looked like, sounded like and was. Oh, I was lyrical. I was dressing all this time, never felt my back once; Herman had done a wonderful job. I walked out, got a tram on the corner up to the station and went home by train; it wasn't all that late. I thought I'd been clever. Wasn't till I got home and found Sophia anxious and miserable at my being away so long that I started feeling rather horrible. I felt horrible for months. I had wronged Sophia, which was the worst. But in a funny way I couldn't help feeling that I'd wronged Elsa too.

'I'd done everything foul you could think of, you see. I'd allowed myself to just sit there and be seduced instead of simply saying thanks and going home. I'd wanted to be seduced, which was bad enough. Then I found an opportunity of working off my own shock at finding myself impotent. I made love that night with Sophia and wasn't in the least impotent. At a guess, it was some psychological block, nothing more. Sleeping then with Sophia was a third crime. All in a row like that it stirred me up considerably.

'I quietened down of course; there were times when I nearly forgot the whole thing, but it worked around in the back of my mind like a needle in the body. Sophia knew too that something was afoot. At first I thought that telling her would be a kind of weakness – a purging myself of guilt, so to speak – and that knowing would make her unhappier. But I couldn't help feeling that the idea was an excuse not to tell her, since I lacked the courage.

'Last week – scarcely a week ago – I made up my mind that I had something to atone for, and that I had better make a proper job of it. I screwed myself up to two actions. The first brought me into the Josef Israelskade. I'd made up my mind simply to go and see her and say that I was sorry. She was intelligent and could be both generous and kind; I hoped that she would accept this – repentance, call it. But it wasn't very easy, and I flummoxed about in the street rehearsing what I was going to say. I wasn't attracted by her any more, and I wasn't frightened of being seduced, but I was nervous.

'I rang the bell, but the door did not open and the speakbox did not answer. I knew she was in – could see the light. I hesitated there perhaps five minutes in all and rang again, might have been in the lavatory or something – still nothing, so I went on. I thought she'd seen me, and refused to answer. Imagined perhaps that I'd come for another shot at making love, who knows? I felt a bit deflated, rather a sense of anticlimax. I went on walking, and planned to write her a letter. I'd intended to tell Sophia everything too; that was the second action. But not having succeeded in the first put me off my stroke a little; I'd about made my mind up to it, the next evening, and then chop! – the boys came in with their big boots.'

The bottle clinked on the edge of the glass.

'*Verdraaid!*' said Van der Valk. 'No more gin in the goddam bottle.' He stood the glass on his nose hopefully to catch the last drops. Putting it down he flexed his fingers.

'My shorthand is so personal I can hardly read it myself. The story is lucid enough anyway, and I think I caught it all. Did you get the Mauriac books, by the way?'

'No, damn it, I forgot them. Would you have remembered?'

'No. I ask as a check on your story. Are they here now?'

'Don't know. Would be in these shelves somewhere if they're here at all. There. Look by the dictionary. You'll find my name in them and a date.'

Van der Valk glanced through one idly. 'Galigai. Wife's name of that pair that made a fool of the king, somehow, in France. Isn't that right?'

'Yes. Concini. The Maréchale d'Ancre.'

'They accused her of being a witch, as I recall, and she said her only witchcraft had been the power of a strong mind over a weaker one?'

'That's her.'

'Would you call that the basis of Elsa's power, too?'

'Number of times I've thought about that. I suppose that is what it boils down to, in the end. You've asked a complex question and the answer would be complex; more to it than that. But I think it's sound enough in my instance. You aren't telling me anything new – I know I'm over-easily influenced. With me, simply, Sophia's character was stronger than Elsa's in the end. That's another story.'

'Yes. Look, you've made a statement, which I've taken down and will ask you to sign. It's evidence in your favour, but it's double-edged; you realize that of course?'

'That was one of the things that held me back. It incriminates me that much deeper, I know, if it isn't true. Because hardly any of it can be proved, except what Herman will tell you.'

'That's what the examining magistrate will say. But true or not it raises an interesting point. Consider this. I quote you more or less verbatim – I didn't get every word you spoke. "The bell did not answer – neither the speakbox. The lights were on, so I knew she was in." A second later – "I thought perhaps she had seen me." Now did you see the curtains move? In a lit room, from the street, you'd have seen her, supposing she looked out of the window.'

'No. Don't even know if the curtains were drawn; think they were, because there was only a faint gleam through the blinds.

'The blinds. Of course. How often these tiny things escape one. With Venetian blinds, of course, one can see out but not in. You see, I came in here and the curtains were closed. I didn't look out. I was here most of the night, what with doctor, photographer and my own thinking. I was back again at nine next morning. Said to the fool of a policeman who was with me, "Get a bit of light into here." Clot pulled the blinds up to the top and I never noticed; I see now. I never thought what light would percolate to the street.'

'Not much. But what's the significance?'

Van der Valk released the blind with a quick jerk and closed it, sloping the slats outward.

'Get a pretty good view of the street if you want, huh? We'll try this at night. From inside, excellent picture of anyone outside. From outside, no shadow visible at all. Stand between the blind and the curtain, and nothing of you will be visible.'

'What makes it important?'

'Look, *jongen*. Maybe she didn't see you. But it's barely possible that someone else did.'

Martin stared.

'If you didn't shoot her,' went on Van der Valk heavily, 'she was shot within half an hour at most of your being here. Strongest presumption: there was someone else with her at the time. Second presumption, pretty strong: it was a lover. Else why not open the door? If it was just friends, you'd open the door, wouldn't you? At the least you'd ask who it was on the squawkbox. You've a pretty strong presumption that it was a lover because she refused to open, and when found – coupled to this – she'd made love within the last few hours. Definite probability to my mind. Whether the examining magistrate would think your story good enough is another matter. But I can start a blitz on her other acquaintances at least. Now first we've got this little affair to clear up.

'I've got to prepare a typed transcript of what you've told

me, which you must agree to and sign. For that we go back to the bureau. First, we wash up like good boys, and destroy evidence of gin. Then I take that statement to the magistrate, with a summary of my findings. On its strength I think I can take time to go through this woman's past life like a dose of salts. If he exists I'll find him – this fancy gunman I mean – not that old cigar-chewer in the Palais. Fix the stove so that it goes out by itself, and leave the window open a crack to air the room. You know something? I keep a policeman out here at night. There is a remote possibility that there is something here that a man might want to come back and get. Sounds remote? But if you've a lover there's bound to be something in your flat, however tiny, that will point to him. Much more likely, of course, that it's somebody sticking out like General de Gaulle in bed with his skis on, and we don't have to crawl about underneath looking for his old slippers.'

Van der Valk was almost at the door of the bureau before he looked Martin in the eye and said, almost affectionately, 'You came up with it all right, *jongen,* but you cut it a bit fine. Now, quick, some food, before any inquisitive bastard smells our breath.'

In the afternoon Martin sat in the detective's office while his statement was typed. This Van der Valk did quite deftly with two fingers, and he only had to search for the rubber once with lazy curses.

'That stupid old Henk can't type at all. Lose the rubber, bound to be him.'

'Did he catch the teddy boy?' asked Martin, interested. It cheered him a little to think that there were after all other crimes and other criminals, and that even the ogrish officer of justice – rapidly becoming a bogy-man even if Van der Valk could talk flippantly about cigar-chewers – could hardly have his beady eye exclusively on Martin.

'That, *jongen,* is police business. Just between you and me and the gas meter he hasn't. But he will. Old Henk grumbles all day, but he's the Sheriff of Tombstone. Always gets his man. He has wonderful pals in cafés. Teddy boys don't go much in cafés and this one's a lone wolf, and not easy to pin down. But old Henk will get him. Eh, does significance end with an "s" or "c"?'

Martin went back to the guardroom at last and fell asleep, but woke up in time for supper; it was cooked sausage that evening, rather fat and not very nice; he was glad of his smoked eel; Sophia had even thought of a lemon to go with it. He stayed in his cell, quite comfortable on the untidy blankets, and was well into the French history – ignominies and iniquities of Louis the Twelfth – before the guard called him.

Sophia looked cold and a little haggard, but her smile was hot and fierce as June sunlight; she did not speak but held out her hands. He kissed both, feeling his heart bumping noisily.

'Before we say anything I've a story I must tell you.' He told it, exactly as he had told it that afternoon. Sophia smoked a cigarette and listened without expression.

'I'm glad you realized, about the atonement.'

'I didn't atone, though.'

'I suppose this is it now. I have to atone also, which does me no harm; I hated that woman so much, and I felt no real remorse even for her death. My guilt is as great as yours. I suppose I have to be grateful that you were impotent with her and not with me; it meant presumably that you loved me. Do you love me still? Or have you concluded that it is her you really love, now that she's dead? Will you feel that she was a martyr to love? Did she die for you? However she died, whoever killed her, it was for you.'

'Darling, what makes you say that?'

'My poor love, how stupid you are. If Van der Valk believes your story – and he does believe it enough, from what you tell me, to make a real search – he does it because there is now a reason for someone else to have killed her. Detach yourself, think of her life. She brought men torment, and no peace. A man was with her; he saw you from the window, recognized you, or she told him who you were. Maybe he knows you. Herman knows you. Munch met you.'

'Munch – that's the fellow's name.'

'Toon knows you. Vogelsang knew you, slightly anyway.'

'Extraordinary thing. I told Van der Valk his name was something like Heemstede.'

'There may be others who know you without your realizing it.'

'Possibly. But knowing me doesn't make him – whoever he is – kill her.'

'I think it could.'

Sophia's rather long, slanting eyes rested on him, objective. 'If you ever, with anyone, deceive me, ever again, I shall go away from you immediately. I will go to another country and no one will be able to find me. Because if I didn't I should certainly kill you; you know me well enough I think to know that I am serious.

'You would not do such a thing, yourself; people like you do not kill; they have too much imagination and their own type of self-control. You stamp and shriek over trifles, but you are quiet in any real crisis. But other men would kill, lacking your control. They have an actuality in their thoughts; they think, "*Écrasez l'infâme*" and they just do it. I could. Somebody like that, suddenly, seeing you, had a horrible certainty. A righteous man perhaps, who thought "This woman must now die," and lost all power over himself except to follow that one impulse. Someone stupid enough never to have realized that she was corrupt, had always been so, and that nothing he could do would change her. My poor darling, not anyone the least like you. Yesterday I was nervous and miserable – I did think for one crazy hour that it was you. Then I knew again that you would not have killed her. Like her, you would have thrown a hairbrush in indignation and wounded pride. You people even look first to see what to throw, and that it isn't something you might be sorry for, afterwards.'

Martin could not stop himself laughing at a characteristic

54

he loved deeply in Sophia. She could not be deceived, even by herself. She was smiling at him now, with self-knowledge.

'Did you enjoy your eel?' Suddenly she gripped him and kissed him hard. 'Thank you for telling. I was afraid you'd try and avoid it – ask Van der Valk to tell me perhaps. I haven't seen him; I don't know what he's thinking but you have, I think, to have confidence in him; he's not so silly and he will have thought of these things. You are very much in his hands, realize.'

Martin remembered this next morning when Van der Valk sent for him to have him finger-printed. He was accustomed by now to the policeman's technique; a talkative flow of confidences, backed by a very shrewd eye that missed little behind what he answered – or did not answer.

'This is all negative. Your prints not being there doesn't eliminate you. A lawyer might present it as a cumulative argument that you were not in the house, but the officer of justice simply shouts that it proves your deep craft and horrid premeditation.

'You're not going to have the pleasure of seeing much of me for a few days. Examining magistrate snorted a good deal over your story; he regards you at present as something crawled out from under a stone – very puritan gentleman sometimes. However, he is a just beast, and he admitted readily that before a case against you could be made any way legal there would have to be exhaustive inquiries. Means I'm exhausted, not him. You stay here. Wheels are going to turn. Lying will begin; all these people are going to say they scarcely knew Elsa's name, or that they saw her only "on business". Frightened of me, frightened of the papers, of the neighbours, of everything imaginable that has nothing to do with right and wrong.'

Martin told him the names Sophia had remembered, and what she had said.

'Interesting woman, your wife. She has the advantage of knowing both you and the lamented Madame de Charmoy

55

very well. Examining magistrate will likely regard her as a promising suspect.' Van der Valk was in his jovial, brutal mood. 'If the fingerprints in the lavatory were yours after all you would be cooked, *jongen*.'

'Ha ha ha,' said Martin sourly.

'Certainly your wife's quite right; there are people always capable of murder and others never really capable. But that's a bit too black-and-white; doesn't take into account the border-line cases and the accidental murderers. This might almost be one of those. No defence in law or anything else. They say they never meant to, and very likely they didn't. Sort of thing means escaping the guillotine in France – always raised with gunshot wounds; clever lawyer can build it up to man-slaughter, even accidental death.

'Guns, you see, are peculiar. A Mauser pistol is a very sensi-tive weapon. If left lying about with the catch off it might go off if you dropped it – automatics are spiteful. One might have murderous ideas, be flourishing the thing about, dramatizing the situation, and it goes off; frightening no one more than the handler. Would explain the running away, though four shots placed together as they were weigh heavily against semi-accidental discharge.

'These are all legal quibbles; don't interest me at all. This gun, now; ballistics boys have got it, seeing if the action is worn or been fiddled with; amusing themselves seeing how much effort it takes to shoot a cardboard man four times in the stomach. They make a hell of a complicated report, all guarded and cautious, which the lawyers quibble over and chew to bits. All meaningless. Go on now; take off.'

Martin spent the day with the League and the battle of Jarnac, and getting sick of Valois princes and the reformed religion, with *Chance* and that indefatigable *raconteur* Marlowe.

In the days to come he was delighted to meet Henk's teddy boy. That gloomy and patient policeman had finally laid his hand on the wrongdoer who had collected old women's handbags. This appalling criminal proved to be a very quiet and nervous boy of an immensely rich and respectable family, and a chess player who could beat Martin three times to two. The boy's devoted mother came every day with things to eat, a fat, gushing woman in magnificent furs, to whom Sophia after an accidental meeting took so violent a dislike that she came late at night thereafter, when everyone was in bed except the guard on night duty.

Martin and the bag-man got three companions, naughty men who had been pinching wood from building sites, and who were always hungry – gladly they ate the despised sausage sent in as rations to the two privileged characters. Martin read French classical authors whom he would probably never have opened otherwise – nothing more readable and interesting in prison than Bossuet and Fénélon. Days passed. The three woodmen were hustled off to the Huis van Bewaring, and the bag-man was closeted endlessly with the very expensive lawyer his family had rushed to capture.

The boy was in a difficult situation, since he was too young to go to any adult prison, and was not the type for an institution of reform. Doubtless the examining magistrate would be wrangling at length with a fine collection of psychiatrists; Martin hoped it would never happen to him.

'Oughtn't you to have a lawyer?' asked Sophia.

'If I need it we'll get one of the free ones.'

'Can't, I inquired. We aren't quite poor enough to be allowed one.'

'Just in the worst situation,' he thought, 'too poor to hire talent, too rich to get any from authority.' He decided to tempt fate and not have any at all.

He annoyed the other prisoners by eating a great deal of garlic with the standard jail brown beans. More days passed. *Chance* was replaced by *Nostromo,* the French history by Fowler, Bossuet by Pascal. With some difficulty he realized that he had been in jail a fortnight.

He was sitting in the guardroom as it drew on towards evening, being a little amazed at the passage of time, when the phone rang on the guard's desk.

'Guardroom,' said that placid gentleman. 'Understood. . . . Van der Valk wants you in the office.'

Martin went, feeling excited and curious; in ten days he had not laid eyes on the detective, and had imagined him occasionally at his little games; shake well before using. He found him sitting at his table, smoking one of his nasty cigarettes, his face as closed as the Stock Exchange on a Sunday.

'Sit down. Got something to tell you at last; may as well say straight away that it isn't what you want to hear.'

He sounded curt and official, and Martin's stomach cramped apprehensively.

'I've gathered all the personnel of the de Charmoy *fabriek* into a bag and stirred thoroughly. Shake well before using.' A small grin from Martin at the accuracy of his imagination, but the policeman went on without noticing. 'Result is exactly zero. The good Herr Munch hasn't been out of Deutschland in the last six months. Your friend Kalkoen claimed he gave her the shove. I'd heard it a bit different, so we had some fun, but he'd enjoyed a good deal of drama anyway. Said she'd threatened to kill herself and that he'd thought that a good idea; asked her to wait till he got a chair so that he could watch such an amusing spectacle in comfort. He'd played some fine games with her all right; once I got him being frank he was even very funny, but it was quite clear that he hadn't seen much of her in the last six months. That's more or less the tale everyone had, and all the dates coincided on this six-months business. The circle was even a good deal narrower than I'd expected. A woman who collects lovers can't expect to have many friends, but she had really lost nearly all hers by simply choking them off. Apart from those who'd lost touch with her altogether, nobody has seen anything of her to speak of in these last months at all. As for information on her life and movements – zero, zero, zero.

'I have to look in a new direction, start one of these awful police routines like showing her picture in pubs. Very lengthy; hell of a lot of cafés in Amsterdam; old Henk could probably tell you the exact number. Good old Henk; he's found a gambling house in the Okeghemstraat. Back to the point; she saw people and people saw her, but nobody belongs in her company. One had coffee with her in Polen; another met her in a print shop in the Voorburgwal. Everyone said her haunt was that bar in the Leidsestraat opposite the American Express; goddam barman remembered her perfectly and had wondered why he hadn't seen her in so long. A new pattern altogether has developed.'

He slapped with an irritated hand on the table.

'I'm not satisfied, because a blank like that with no man showing regularly alongside does not accord with what I understand of her. As I see her, she took her Teddy bear with her 'most everywhere.'

Van der Valk kept silent a moment, studying Martin's face. He seemed to make up his mind about something.

'You know what he says, the magistrate? That the fact that nobody shows alongside her only means that whoever was, to use his foul phrase, "consorting with her" did not wish to be seen with her and took pains to be discreet. And who is it? He's quite sure that it's you. He's told me to get you charged and brought in to him. He said a good deal more too.'

'Isn't that enough?'

'Yes ... enough for you ... but already too much for me. He was disagreeable. Said I'd handled you all wrong; allowed you to have too much information, that enabled you to fabricate a story which we could not readily disprove. Quoted the rule-book: investigating officers must not depart from established methods of interrogation. Discretion must at all times be left to judgment of superior officers. In other words, don't use your brain. Be a farmer holding a stop-and-go sign outside the Hôtel Victoria. He said if he failed to get a judgment against you he would feel that the police methods used were responsible. That you were quite evidently carrying on behind your wife's back and that he, repeat he, knew perfectly well how to put the matter beyond doubt.

'I don't know why the *godverdomme* hell I'm telling you this, but I told him that I might be a bum policeman but that I'd seen you and he hadn't. You see, *jongen*, whether I like you or not has nothing to do with my job. Can't do any good at this trade if you start liking or disliking people. But I'm an honest fool, and I don't particularly want to see you screwed when I honestly don't think you killed her. Now you've got me on the shit-list, but I'm not backing out on my own judgment. I'm not thinking this crime is solved because you're all set to step off for it.

'I have, oddly enough, just a little private, human, quiet reason of my own. You know, *jongen*, I have more diplomas and law-books under my belt than the minister of justice has in his goddam panelled office, and I earn about as much as a post-office clerk. But if I can unwind this cute little affair I'm in line for the higher *échelon*, get me? Make my wife happy as well as yours, huh?' He allowed himself one thin, tight smile, and looked at his watch. 'It's six-thirty. Have you eaten?'

'Yes.'

'Then come; you and I are going to pay another little visit to the Josef Israelskade.'

On the way out he spoke a few words to the brigadier on duty. 'I'm taking them off this watch. If there's anything in that flat to find I intend to find it tonight. We've got to shift gears.' Outside, along the still water, he intercepted a loitering figure that sloped off thankfully.

'All ours now,' Van der Valk opened the door and hurried Martin in. The room was the same, but shabbier. Dust was gathering now; the air felt a little musty and damp.

'Will you clear the stove and light it?'

While Martin was busy, he prowled through the flat, peering at doors, running a fastidious finger along dusty edges. He came back wiping his hands.

'We can say fairly certainly that nobody has been here. Just for luck I'd done the talcum-powder trick on the doors.' He took his coat off slowly and sat down rubbing his nose with a gesture familiar by then to Martin.

'I think that the secret of all this, if that isn't too much of a word. lies here in this street, in this house. It all springs from here. In this room I can smell the hanky-panky.' He warmed himself at the stove. 'This is a question of character. Her character. She was a secretive woman. Everything she did, when she could make it so, was underhand, designed to deceive and to mislead. She did it all her life as far as I can see. Now that she's dead she's trying to convince me that she was only a harmless woman getting on into middle age, deserted by her husband, forced to earn a living. Only interested in her work. finding a quiet means of life instead of all the storms and whirlpools. Picking up perhaps with an old lover as she got biologically a little stirred up, approaching menopause and how-are-you. I think all this is a lie.' He sounded as though he had a personal grievance against Elsa. He too, thought Martin, has come under the spell.

'Lies, like all the other lies. The woman lied to everyone, including herself. Lying to me now, telling me that everything is above board, everything is easy, just as the examining magistrate thinks.

"Look," he says, "nine times out of ten and more the solution is the obvious, straightforward, self-evident explanation." Quite true too. "There this man is with everything; means, opportunity and motive, just like the book says, and you're trying to tell me that it's your goddam old friend Mister X. Now bring this fellow in. Hammer him. We'll get the truth." Now I'm the joker in the pack, who doesn't believe that it's like that, because of this woman. I don't believe their nice easy solution. I think it's a lie. A lie that she's telling me.'

His eyes flicked continually round the room, as though a

mouse might at any moment pop out of a mousehole. Martin said so, and he laughed.

'That's it; you follow me. This woman hid things. She wrote things down, as though she needed to have nuts put away like a squirrel. Letters, diaries, do I know what; the flat is full of her writing. Now, we've no proof of the existence of Mister X, but if I've understood this woman at all she left one, and I'm going to spend the whole night if need be finding it.'

'What about the policeman, or better still the neighbours? Have they seen nobody, before or since? What about that *verdomde* old woman who saw me?'

Van der Valk laughed.

'You don't forgive that old woman, do you? She's the common everyday window-peeper of course, with nothing to do except watch other people. Useful sometimes. This one's a perfect type; widow of a seed merchant, comes from the backwoods god-knows-where in Overijssel, and behaves as though she'd never left. Except for these old women Amsterdammers aren't as a rule nosy about their neighbours. In The Hague everyone knows everyone's business; possibly; so they say. It doesn't work that way here. I've had to rely on that old woman more than I could wish, and she's seen nothing. Nothing then – Elsa knew how to be discreet ("He's calling her Elsa now," thought Martin with a grin) – and nothing since – at least, no strangers seen hanging about in any sense. All the people who live in the district she knows by heart, and most of their visitors too.

' "There's the mother who lives in Dordrecht, up for the day, be sure; isn't it their wedding anniversary? There is the sister, the one that's married to the doctor in Bussum; he must be doing well and spending it on her, that handbag is real crocodile. There's the Jansens' little girl – isn't she late today getting back from school? And there's the boyfriend with the big American car; now what does he pretend to do for a living?" All taped you see.

'Of course, she knew Elsa had all sorts of friends; seen her

at one time or another with half my photo-gallery. But – again
– none for some months. And only in daylight, of course, she
doesn't operate at night. Whereas Elsa did. Old Afterdark de
Charmoy. I haven't got a thing out of any of these people, but
here is where we'll find what there is.' He was clearing the
books off the shelves.

'Go through each book; don't just shake, but make sure
there's nothing tucked away, even a slip of paper. Put those
that have been done on the other rug, there, in a pile.' He
emptied the shelves and began methodically and unsmilingly
poking at crevices.

'I'll take all that antique furniture to bits, if need be. Some
of those things have trick drawers, but they're generally easy
to spot. The back off all the pictures, all the carpets up, everything. She may well have thought of some quite clever ideas,
but they won't stand up to a professional search, and that's
what I mean to give this place.'

Half an hour later he said: 'There's no gin, and only a few
grains of coffee left, but we'll have some tea when we've
finished this room.'

A little later he said: 'Go on, talk. This is going to take
maybe five hours, perhaps more. Talk. About anything. No, not
about anything; tell me about her. I intend to get inside this
woman's mind. Tell me how you met her, how you got to become her lover, how you parted, the lot. Think that you're on
the lovely black leather couch and that I'm there with the
soothing smile and the nice syringe full of pentothal. Go on;
talk.'

Martin talked. It came easily; rambling and disconnected,
punctuated by tea, and cigarettes, and more tea, and Van der
Valk's merciless hands taking things to pieces. Everything in
the studio and kitchen as it was examined was brought into
the living-room and stacked neatly. He took the gramophone
to pieces, and the back off the radio. The pelmets came off the
curtains, the shades off the lamps, and with her belongings
Elsa's life was taken apart and inspected gravely.

Martin began with his first, half-forgotten meetings with her, fifteen years before, often muddling details and occasions, going back to correct and fill in, remembering now jokes, catchwords, scraps of conversations, uproarious amusement and furious shame. Van der Valk seemed sometimes not to be listening as he dismembered and sifted, but he never lost his concentration, and asked questions frequently. Martin had no idea how long it lasted; his voice got tired and he stopped to think and forgot to go on, staring in memory.

Once Van der Valk interrupted to play some records that seemed suspect, but they were all music; music that reminded him of other times that he and Elsa had sat together in a warm, lamplit room playing records.

It was growing at last to the end of the search, which had produced nothing but old envelopes, forgotten lipsticks, pencils, a broken cigarette lighter, many needles, and twists of string. Van der Valk was in the bedroom, stripped now and blank, with Martin sitting on the bare springs of the bed. The room had yielded nothing, any more than the others, but the policeman showed no sign of impatience and few of fatigue; he was fiddling with the big dressing-table.

'This wood is solid as a house,' he muttered, 'no point in trying to take this to pieces.'

He tilted the centre glass thoughtfully back and forward, and stared down at the dusty table-top, clear now of junk. Suddenly he stared into the glass, alert; Martin thought he was looking at his own face and made a bad joke. He put up both hands and gripped the glass by the edges. His thumbs went to the steel clasps that bound them; they slid outwards. Very carefully Van der Valk pressed the others out, gripped the heavy, fine old glass and slid it up and away from the wooden backing. Martin watched without any particular interest. With a sudden loud flap an envelope hit the floor, as though a hidden postman had just popped it through the box.

'Ah,' said Van der Valk, picked it up and put it in his pocket. 'Looking-glasses are interesting things, and when they get old reflect more than the face that looks in them. I think it must have amused her to look at her secrets every time she looked at her face. "There are my secrets, behind my face; read them who can." Typical of her, really; stupid of me not to have followed that mind, now that I know something of its working. Go on with your story; we aren't finished yet.'

One of the side glasses yielded a second envelope, which joined the first, but the rest of the search was fruitless. Back in the living-room Van der Valk rubbed his eyes, fumbling a cigarette out with his free hand, and sat down.

'Surely there's a bottle somewhere.' He did not move to get it. 'I've had worse days; it's only half past one. What's in it?'

'Apricot brandy. Same she gave me when I was last here.'

'I'll drink to that occasion.' He brought out the envelopes and opened them. Each held a dozen or so postcard-sized photographs; he studied them, his face wooden; he did not show them to Martin. When he looked up he had a broad grin and his eyes were alive with good humour behind the dusty curtain of fatigue.

'I'm glad you told that story; interests me very much ... I hope I never have to come here again ... Got you now, my girl, now I have you.'

On the way back to the bureau he spoke only once.

'What was the name again of the street where she lived, when you met her?'

'Matthew Marisstraat,' answered Martin. 'Number eighty-seven.'

Part Two

Matthew Marisstraat 87

He knew it first in the now scarcely remembered days just after the war. His memory was vague because everything was so meaningless; he was still in uniform, and men from every imaginable unit were muddled together in obscure places performing ludicrous actions, because there was nothing else for them to do. People who had shaken at the sight of a German soldier for five years were marching about, busy and self-important with unnecessary guns, arresting great numbers of so-called collaborators. Dim personages emerged as partisan heroes and abrogated authority; others returned hastily from safe refuges and pretended they had been in the *maquis*. Very many private scores were quietly paid off; there was a lot of pious looting of the property '*des amis de Fritz*'.

Martin was sent from Strasbourg to Amsterdam, since people in uniform who could speak four languages were rare. Enterprising soldiers had by this time developed the ignoring of authority to a complex and exacting art. People who had a talent for it laid the foundation of future fortunes; Martin disobeyed silly orders for fun, because it would make no difference to anyone, and because it meant inventing amusing and ridiculous lies.

He was attached to a formation supplying largely non-existent supplies, and instructed to detect and suppress the black market. This was largely an English enterprise, and he was rather out of place. Technically a French soldier, wearing an American uniform, a Dutch citizen in Holland, nobody could quite fit him into the worthy British pattern of anterooms and orderly rooms; he lived a frivolous and rather drunken life.

There was any amount of work but everybody was too busy purging the body politic to do it. There were of course very many devoted and sensible people in Holland who were working very hard to restore a disrupted economy and heal the wounds of hatred and bitterness, but with the whole world centred on the nasty farce being prepared at Nuremberg people on the whole did not realize that political vengeance, reprisal and dismantling are singularly useless at feeding hungry people. Martin knew perfectly well that it is hopeless to do anything about a black market in a shortage of everything that ordinary people want, and relapsed into total disillusionment. He was just twenty-one years old.

He was trying to find a three-ton lorry-load of food that had disappeared behind clouds of lies somewhere near Apeldoorn, when he saw a familiar sight by the side of the road, and stopped the jeep. A girl, staring rather hopelessly at a bicycle with a flat tyre. It was an old, sad bicycle, loaded with two sacks arranged as panniers, holding quite a lot of apples and potatoes. The girl had been crying but was calm. Martin did not perhaps care about black markets, but he lent what help he could to people who were hungry. He shook his head over the tyre.

'Cooked. I can put my finger through the tube anywhere. Where do you want to go?'

'Amsterdam.'

He was not surprised; these things had been common since the hungry winter of forty-four. 'Well, it's easy enough as it happens; you can ride with me.'

She shook her head.

'No? Don't be silly; I'm an Amsterdammer like you, and haven't any ideas of raping anyone. I'll put the bike in the back.'

'Are you married?' he asked twenty miles further. 'I see your ring, but is that camouflage or *echt*?'

'*Echt*,' with a bitter little smile. 'I have two children, and my husband's in prison.'

'Why?'

'No why, except he's half German, and there's a big witch-hunt going on. Not collaborator, nothing, except trying to earn a living, and some can't forgive that.'

'Where do you live?'

'I'd rather not say if you don't mind.'

He understood; she was extremely pretty; hunger had made her beautiful.

'Where do you want me to drop you? Lairessestraat is where we go.'

'That will be all right.'

He had put her down and she had plodded off pushing the flat bicycle and the sack of vegetables, not looking back. Determined and independent. He shrugged; the town was full of such chance meetings as well as such stories. People competed with horrors and hard-luck stories. Ten years later half Amsterdam was to have its own particular 'Anne Frank' legend.

When, hardly a fortnight later, he saw her queueing for bread in the Vermeerstraat he realized that chance had taken a hand, stayed where he was, and followed discreetly. Matthew Marisstraat. Number eighty-seven. He rang; her face was hard with anger.

'I know, I know; I only saw you quite by accident at the baker. I'm not chasing you; I only wanted to ask whether I mightn't – well, call on you; sounds silly I know. When it suited you. No strings.' He tried to recover his self-possession.

'I suppose that if I don't let you in you'll keep coming back and pestering me.'

'That's right.'

'It'll choke you off the quicker then if I say right now that I'm not to be had; not with coffee, not with chocolate, not with anything.'

'Makes no difference to me.'

'Come in,' she said, abrupt.

It was three high, but light and airy. Two small children were playing on the floor.

'Sit down,' politely. 'I can't make you coffee anyway; I haven't any. Look, there are plenty who'd be only too glad. Can't you see you're wasting your time?'

He nodded peacefully and offered her a cigarette, which she took. 'I've persuaded you to take something, anyhow. Don't be so certain that I'm just after you either; there are other things in the world.' Feeling he sounded a bit priggish he strolled over to the long row of shelves. 'Do you think it would be all right if I borrowed a book some time?'

She smiled then, a genuine one.

'I think that would be all right,' she parodied. 'Take one if you like.'

He chose an old Sinclair Lewis – *Arrowsmith*. She lifted her eyebrows but said nothing.

'I can't stay now; I'm supposed to be working. Thank you very much indeed.'

He came back three days later with two army blankets, a bottle nearly half-full of whisky, and a large tin of peaches.

'Did you like *Arrowsmith*?'

'Mad on it.'

They were friends.

He got in the habit of often dropping in, never staying long, when he had 'won' anything desirable. When he had coffee she made some, and he sat in one of the big old-fashioned armchairs and they talked books, and he would take three or four when he left. After a few weeks he was at home enough to play with the children, and had learned her name: Elsa.

She was nearly five years older than he was; she was twenty-five and had been married three years. A friend of her father's lived near Apeldoorn – in forty-four he had just about kept them alive, and she had made the trip nearly every week. Her husband was a sort of archaeologist – he understood old manuscripts and inscriptions – and before the war had had a good research job in Munich. But here in Amsterdam he had no work at present, and life was by no means easy.

She sat on the floor during these conversations, cross-legged in an old pair of corduroy trousers and wooden-soled sandals; she had pretty undistorted feet. He liked the feeling of home; of soup cooking and nappies drying and 'women's things'; he liked as well the feeling of civilization, a love of conversation which it seemed to him had disappeared everywhere else. Sometimes they sat still for a whole evening listening to a concert on the radio, or reading, or simply saying nothing; silence except for the click of knitting needles. He ate with her too, but never without having brought a contribution – corned beef, condensed milk, a treasure sometimes like fruit or bacon. She accepted everything naturally, without gush – neither thanks, protests nor any show of emotion, though she did not bother to hide her pleasure, and a rarity like soap would make her laugh and make a little grimace of enjoyment.

She did not talk often about her husband, or with much enthusiasm; he was too fond of gin, she let fall. They never got involved in any closer relationship than this; he kissed her hand when he came in, and otherwise did not touch her, nor did she leave the bedroom door open, or show herself half-dressed. There was no familiarity on either side; he did not really know why this was but was quite happy that things should stay so. It certainly did not seriously occur to him to try to seduce her; he told himself that he respected her. Once he took her to Apeldoorn again, for apples.

It was a lovely warm autumn day, and she was happy at being in the country, and enjoying the still clean air and the warm orchard smell. She was wearing shorts she had made from an old curtain, and had climbed the tree. He stood below, catching the apples she tossed him and stowing them in a basket. As he glanced up at her, balanced in a fork six feet above his head, he noticed that the hollow of her thigh and the mount of Venus were in full view. When she climbed down he had a strong desire to throw her in the long grass, but he did no such thing. Maybe he was nervous of spoiling a friendship that had come to mean a lot to him, since, he considered, she would certainly resist and be angry. He soon forgot the incident, and his little physical memory of her did not worry him.

He liked her frankness; she was straightforward and unambiguous. She appealed to some sense of chivalry in him; he was very young. A sort of comradeship grew between them. He was proud to be with her, and liked looking at her. She was worth looking at; she had magnificent legs, and a good figure, a thought too heavy. Her features, to him, were of an unequalled beauty; they had, indeed, the Garboesque cast that is exceedingly attractive. Her bad, ugly hands seemed to him piquant and amusing. When tired or excited she had a violent nervous twitch; it never worried him, though he was sorry for her. Her hair was bright blonde, long and had a slight wave; she wore it pinned up on top of her head, and he liked best to see her in the classic pose, her arms up, pinning it in place with a frown of concentration. It was a good life, and did not last long enough.

The army sent him back to France, where he kicked his heels for three months in Rouen before being released. When he came again to Amsterdam, it was a year after he had seen her first. He had written two books, and a friend of his North African army days had good relations with a Paris publishing house. His first was an angry attack on the American military administration, which had been very tiresome towards the French troops under its nominal command; it did well in France. His publisher persuaded him that being anti-American was amusing and fashionable in France but did not make much money, and his second was a reversal – wild melodrama full of horrid Russians and the sinister shadows of blackmarketeers everywhere. The Americans enjoyed it greatly, and it made a film. It hardly sold a copy in France, but lovely dollars clinked in his pocket. Both books were called by some farcical, by others cynical, by others satirical – he liked those best. They made him quite a reputation, and he was well able to stay in Paris, but it was not a gay city in the early days of forty-seven. Neither was Amsterdam, but Elsa was there.

He had written her two or three long letters, full of ideas and descriptions, inconsequential and amused. She had answered with a careful criticism of both books, serious and well-reasoned. There was very little personal in these letters. They were like their conversations; she made a bare mention of the fact that her husband had been released, and, possibly to compensate for unusually unjust and stupid handling, that he had got a job in the Museum, not terribly highly paid but secure, quiet, and good for his health. He felt excitement, and anticipatory pleasure at the thought of seeing her.

When he arrived it pleased him that everything was quite unchanged – she had bought a few things and her clothes were less obviously home-made, but the flat had still its pre-war curtains and shabby furniture, and she still sat on the floor. The biggest difference was that he brought things to drink now instead of to eat.

Her husband surprised him. Erich was fifteen years older than her and looked twenty. He was a very tall, thin man with a quiet voice; nervous and shaky, and given to obscure jokes. Martin rather liked him.

He was in her house now three or four days a week; he had little to do, apart from his girls. There was something nowadays to amuse him besides herself; she had made many friends, and the company would sit till late in her living-room. There was something of a salon in the Matthew Maris at week-ends. Three or four men, with a silent and rather puzzled girl friend or two, would drink tea – none of them were rich – and flail away happily at philosophy. Big Henry Ruysbroeck, the journalist with the beard, in public ferocious and polemical, a pen that dripped blood, in private a mild man, fondest of food. Paul de Vries, a young actor, rather sick of being thought promising, who went on about Eduard Verkade till everyone was a little bored. Bert van Roij, the Limburger who was trying to earn a living as a painter – 'but follow at present in the illustrious footsteps of Adolf' – and Priscilla, the English girl who looked like Queen Nefertiti in the Berlin Museum. Ginette Valdes, who played the piano in a restaurant and hated it like poison, but knew she was not really good enough for a concert stage. Elsa had for them all, it seemed, the same detached friendship.

Martin came more often than any, preferably when no one else was there. It was rare for Erich to be home till midnight; he undoubtedly drank a great deal, though when he did appear he was only noticeably more vague and absent-minded, and occasionally sarcastic, but not quarrelsome or truculent. He had his own mysterious friends, with whom he played chess and talked opera, his two great passions.

Martin learned to come on slack days, and enjoy the stillness.

'What was it like in your father's house?' he asked. This was the day after Paul, who had socialist leanings, had begun: 'Troelstra said . . .'

Henry interrupted. 'Damnation to all socialists, but foremost and especially Pieter Jelles Troelstra.'

A tremendous row developed.

'Attlee I admire to some extent, the extent that his head rules his heart.'

'Attlee!' said Priscilla, as though the name was blasphemous and obscene.

'Not a socialist at all. Laski if you like –'

'Laski,' said Henry rhetorically, 'is' –there was a rush of interruption, but 'flatulent . . . decomposed . . . outdated . . . undigested . . .' could be heard through the din. Elsa quelled a spitting Priscilla.

'Please don't ever talk politics in my house; too boring, and reminds me of my father's house much too vividly.'

'Dreadful,' she answered now to Martin's question. 'Very vulgar and ostentatious, *bourgeois* as could be, a sort of Friesian Forsyte, provincial and narrow-minded, rich in a thoroughly useless way. Father paid lip-service to conventions, and only broke them on the sly, beginning by sleeping with both his sisters-in-law. In the end, even he couldn't live it down. He ran away to Brussels; I went to boarding-school there. My mother died of tuberculosis about a year after; I was nine at the time.'

'Is he still in Brussels?'

'I've no idea; haven't seen him since thirty-nine. I wrote to him when I got married; he sent me those Toorop drawings – the ones Bert is so rude about – as a wedding present, and a letter full of morality. Admonishing me to be a faithful wife.'

'And you are?'

'Yes, but believe me, not because of my upbringing. It might surprise the crowd I used to run with. When I was seventeen I ran away from school and came here. I was Lesbian then. Nymph, they used to call me.'

'What did you do?'

'Artist's model. Nude, of course, all the time. There are pictures of me nude in half the old men's bedrooms in Aerdenhout.'

'Bah!'

'Why "Bah"? It's not me. None of them were even good pictures.'

'And did you sleep with the artists?'

'A good many of them, I suppose. Didn't notice much; I was drunk all the time in those days. I do recall losing my virginity, though; I was sixteen, in Davos for the winter sports. He was a Hitler Jugend boy called Heinz; perfect healthy type, brown like coffee, hair bleached nearly white, wonderful skier and proud like a Caesar at seventeen years old. Exact *Übermensch;* he just looked at me and said: "Take your clothes off and lie in the snow," and of course I did.'

'Wasn't it cold?' said Martin, laughing hard.

'Very, but the sun is hot. If you've never been you can't imagine.'

Martin was not much surprised, nor bothered, by these

tales. It was not till many years later that he realised that they were a pack of lies. Not really a dramatized fantasy; the truth cannot have been so dissimilar, but simply lying for the sake of excitement, mystification, seduction.

'Of course,' he told Sophia ten years later, 'I was supposed to say too, "Take your clothes off and lie in the snow." She must have thought me a perfect eunuch.' At the time his trust and belief in Elsa were complete.

He had already long understood that she was not a quiet little housewife, and was pleased, since it would have been boring. Her virtue was heroic to an idealistic boy. It made her stillness and calm remarkable, and her housewife's life had more dignity with the background of a stormy youth sketched in. If she was in a talkative mood she would tell stories sometimes of this still recent past.

'Most of the men of that time are dead.' Several had gone to concentration camps; one lover, a beloved painter, had died of tuberculosis. Another had been executed by partisans and she had escaped with a shaved head and the word 'whore' in red paint on her breast and back, but the chief of that band had been her next lover, to be executed in his turn by the Germans.

Martin understood that she was a woman with whom all men fell in love, and a woman who brought men very easily to their deaths. He could understand that they might even have found death worth while. In some way he was exempt, it seemed, from this ruinous passion; what he felt for her was not love, was it?

She was not very interested in sex, either.

'I have been raped too often in my life, and I dread the luck-ily rare occasions when Erich has not had enough to drink, and recovers a remnant of interest in my body. I do not much like making love.'

'How did you come to marry him?'

'He picked me up half starving and stupid with gin. He took me home, washed me, fed me, dressed me, cared for me and gave me a home. I have not yet lost my gratitude to him. He raped me, naturally, but that only became important when I found myself pregnant. We married; he offered because of the child; I accepted because I wished to be clean. I stopped drinking; when you gave me a cigarette the first time you were here it was my first in three years.'

'And why did you take it then?'

'I did not want to hurt you. You looked so vulnerable and lonely.'

Martin swallowed this nonsense whole.

He had found a flat, or so it was called. It was one good big room in the Emmastraat, with a tiny kitchen and lavatory on the landing. He cleaned it himself, occasionally. His instinct for a home was strong; he bought books and pictures, and had a treasured Tabriz carpet. He kept his souvenirs here, a night-glass of the type issued to U-boat captains, and a Mauser pistol; his tools, typewriter, notebooks and a Paris telephone directory; and his pleasures, odd bottles of expensive vintage wine, and letters from girls. This room gave him enormous pleasure.

Often he changed the position of all the furniture; often he read and drank coffee till four in the morning. His cave. Nobody came here except girls – who came in a long procession. Elsa never came, nor did he ask her. He was satisfied with life; he went to theatres, cinemas, concerts, galleries; he sat on café terraces, drank Pernod, and listened to the band. He did no work, and finally Elsa tackled him.

'You do nothing.'

'I do. I have at least two notebooks full of material.'

'Two notebooks full of whores' addresses. You sit around all day; you eat and drink too much. It's too easy for you; you've got soggy; you must get something done or you'll lose all the ground you've made. I think that you're too introspective, and certainly too dependent on me. Think about it. Oh, I know that you have endless excuses; it's always a headache or a bad throat or too hot or too cold; you have rheumatism or your scar aches. But I notice that none of these things stop you making love to rather unsuitable girls.'

He disregarded these remarks for a week, in rather a sulk, before getting a letter from his publisher. Where was his new book? His sales had fallen off badly, the public was forgetting he existed, and the golden flow of dollars was a thing as good as finished.

Martin looked at his last statement from the bank, a thing he had not done in a year, and got a fearful fright. He stormed over to the Matthew Maris.

'The trouble is,' he was saying an hour later, 'that I can't really work here at all. I've tried three or four times to make a start, put a thousand words or so on paper – seemed all right at the time but when I woke up next morning it was just tripe – straight into the waste-paper basket. So I'm going to Paris.'

'Sooner the better,' said Elsa, placidly biting off her thread. Martin sulked behind a newspaper for most of the evening, but went to Paris next day.

His army friend was living in Meaux, which is a boring little town but handily near Paris, and had gone into transport; he owned a fleet of wagons now and a wife. Catherine was thirty, and had a flexible, cuddly body and a kind and willing nature. Max had said, 'Let's go to Cannes for the week-end' – damn the fellow, he had pots of money. He did not notice when Martin seduced Catherine, largely because he did not care. Nevertheless, Martin was ashamed of himself. The feeling of remorse, worthy if belated, was helped perhaps by his having no money left. He did not dare to face his publisher, but took a job for a season as a waiter; it was a success.

In the autumn he found he had saved enough to live three months at least, and did, in a *pension* at winter terms at St. Jean de Luz, where he was greatly bitten by fleas, got drunk a couple of times in Perpignan, and finished his book in six weeks on a funny little old-fashioned Corona with a beautiful typeface. It was a satire on the tourist industry, not very good, but his publisher forgave him. He had not the nerve to go back to Meaux, but hung around for a week in Paris, feeling rather at a loss. It was nearly Christmas, and he felt a rush of homesickness. He got on to the Paris-Amsterdam express with a feeling of happiness, which began to sing inside him when they crossed the border. Holland is clean and sparkling after the gloom of industrial Belgium, at any time. In the Emmastraat at last, he told himself, he would have a light heart.

When he got there, it was not quite so good. His precious objects looked ordinary and trivial, almost trashy. There was a good deal of dust. Even his carpet looked dingier than he remembered it. The electricity had been cut off, and he had to grovel in the faint glimmer of the street for an oil lamp. No gas either; he had to wash in cold water.

'Typical of me to have forgotten'; a postcard would have fixed it all, but there – he shrugged – his character was like that; a thing like a journey was no fun unless you did it at a moment's notice. When he went out to a restaurant the food was vile; the *schnitzel* tasted like donkey and the beans were overcooked. He felt fed up, and jarred, and slept badly; the sheets felt damp and everything stank of disuse; having foreseen that was small satisfaction.

Disillusionment persisted next day in the Matthew Marisstraat; a stranger was sitting in the chair he thought of as his. A tall, broad-shouldered man, a year or two older than himself, with long dark hair, a self-satisfied look, and eyes the colour of weak coffee. English; his name was Kenneth MacPherson. A radio producer, in the tow of Arie Vogelsang; it seemed he had a year's contract with one of the television companies in Bussum. Martin took an immediate strong dislike to this personage, and went into the kitchen to talk to Elsa.

She had changed, not much but definitely; her hair was cut; she talked more and faster, and she seemed nervous.

'We can't stay out here, it's very rude. And talk English; Kenneth knows no Dutch.'

'Hadn't he better start learning if he's going to be here a year?'

'Oh, the radio people are like the airlines; international communication – they all talk English. Come on, let's be civilized for once. We don't have to talk Dutch; this isn't the opening of the States General.'

He was surprised; it was an affected and stupid remark, quite unlike her. At supper she not only spoke English but put milk in Martin's tea; 'Hey,' he said.

She laughed lightly. 'Sorry, I forgot.'

Mr MacPherson took milk in his tea. He had, as well, a deep, throaty voice. But he was polite to Martin.

'I remember your book about the black market. Very good, I thought it. I'm not too keen about the Americans myself, though of course in television they're technically ahead of us. How was Paris? I'm always promising myself to take a proper holiday and really get to know Paris.'

'Speak French?'

'Well, school French, you know.'

'Ah. Well it's like here; people do talk English if it's called for.'

'Yes, everybody speaks English now, I imagine.'

'Even if it's with an American accent,' said Martin, a thought spitefully. He had decided that Mr MacPherson was a perfect peasant.

A few years later the poor fellow came on holiday and visited old friends. Sophia met him at a party in Elsa's house; she confirmed Martin's view: 'A real clown; all hands, feet and big mouth. Had the cheek to write me a little note saying how struck he was with my charms, in the most illiterate handwriting you could imagine.' But at the time Martin put his dislike down to his own injured vanity. It did not please him to be taking second place in Elsa's house.

'How's Henry?' he asked casually.

'I haven't seen him for a few months.'

'Is he ill?'

'I don't know. He does go on so; we've lost touch in a way.'

'Hm,' thought Martin, 'Mr Thing has put everybody off, be sure.'

It did not put him off, though. The question never came up, since he had hardly been home a week before a new scheme was occupying him. His publisher wrote saying that the translation of his tourist book was going well in England, and enclosing a polite letter from the editor of a weekly newspaper in London, with a tentative commission for a series of outlined articles. Martin, finding life in the Matthew Maris did not include him at all, gratefully took a plane to London.

It was fascinating; he knew that the English literary landscape was a paradox, but he had imagined nothing like what he found. People, in enormous numbers, were interested in books and making a tremendous business out of it. They might, admitted, be not much good at the other arts, but with books – astonishing. Hundreds of publishers, innumerable magazines, double the number of weeklies one found anywhere else. Critics gave books serious attention and a huge amount of column space. There was no nonsense about a Prix Femina or anything else. And what a language! Enormously rich, flexible and subtle. Martin's English was not, though it was fluent, idiomatic and fairly accurate, and he was rather cast down by the infinitely fine gradations of sense. He worried over Fowler and Ivor Brown and Eric Partridge, and threw his efforts at writing English in the waste-paper basket.

The commissioned articles were one of those Changing Face of Europe slants: 'Everywhere beside the raw bomb-craters the curves and planes of vigorous new blah blah express the determination blah . . .' and so on. Martin went to see his editor in a depressed mood.

'Perhaps you'd better get a translator. The more I look at my English the more inaccurate I see it.'

'Perhaps I'd better get André Maurois,' said the editor jovially; he was one of those beefy Englishmen with a club tie and a huge moustache, with which he wore a bowler hat.

'I don't want it particularly accurate; my whole idea was to write about Europe in a European idiom. Something that has a European flavour and inflection. Forget all that Fowler stuff; that will just make you self-conscious. The whole point about your English is that even if you use a cliché it doesn't sound like one.'

Martin found that he was quite a success. People asked him to their houses, to stay; they had great hospitality. He got introductions everywhere in the literary network; he got a dozen small commissions, reviewing Simenon, a translation of Molière – rather good – and a long essay following a new biography of Conrad, dealing with the 'European' novels. He enjoyed himself greatly; he wrote a novel in English and had a love affair with an English girl called Diana. Mr MacPherson might, possibly, be making conquests in Holland, but he would get his own back here.

He even lost his head rather over Diana, went too far and asked her to marry him. She very luckily refused, for the excellent reason that she did not think she would be happy in another country. Since she was the most English girl that ever wore a Braemar twin-set this was sensible of her. He was not that anglicized. When she asked him whether he would stay in England he said, rather rudely, 'Good God, no.' That did it. And indeed the gilt wore off the gingerbread (he greatly enjoyed such phrases, what on earth did they mean? – English was a fascinating language) very quickly.

The novel was not much of a success. English people enjoy being laughed at. Had he been a wee tiny bit too condescending? His articles were accepted and paid for, he appeared on television and was quoted in a 'Things they Say' column ('English homes are delightful; such a pity that the furniture is always so dreadful') – but he caused no great stir, and the tourist articles, which had been announced with a flourish, petered out a bit.

The control on the amount of money that one could take out of England was, at that time, severe: the English as a whole are anyway not interested in Europe. They do not regard their island as part even of the European continent; they talk of 'the Continent', meaning elsewhere. The articles were admittedly quite clever and amusing; everyone said so, and praise was voluble; Martin was conscious, however, of a slight dull thud somewhere.

But he was well pleased to live six months in the country, and he got a great deal out of studying English. He made discoveries, such as that 'geyser' was surely the same as the Dutch 'gozer' and that, surprisingly, many people thought his Dutch accent sounded Scotch. Why did they talk about a biscuit, when the Americans use the Dutch word cookie? And there was such a lot to read. *Sunday Times* and *Spectator, New Statesman* and *Tablet, Punch* and *Listener, Literary Supplement* and Sotheby's catalogue.

Dickens he liked greatly, once he learned to skip. Mr Chadband was a model surely for Elmer Gantry, and he was entranced with Mr Mantalini, and Captain Cuttle. The gold of English phrase – Sam Weller and Silas Wegg – made him drunk. Like Mr Polly he went round murmuring 'portly capon' and 'chinking, twinkling, demd mint sauce'.

There were good and bad things everywhere. Yorkshire pudding was dreadful but horseradish nice; so was red currant jelly. The porridge was dread but the Cooper's Oxford bliss (he found it difficult to stop using Mitford baby-talk). Beer was difficult – how did one drink this soupy stuff? – but whisky was marvellous. Smashing.

'Look, one doesn't say A-one, nor smashing, nor capital, nor super.'

'Well, what does one say?'

He enjoyed afternoon tea: 'I-don't-take-milk-in-Holland-but-I-do-here.'

'You could say just Good. If it was very good, you could say Marvellous. Not fabulous – only in advertisements. Marvellous would do.'

'Like that, with a bleat?'

'If you insist.'

'I won't bleat. Won't say marvellous any more than actually. I shall say Less Bad, like the Spanish.'

'I must admit, Martin, that for a foreigner . . .'

It was not till he was back in Paris that he wondered how on earth he had stuck it so long.

It was more habit than anything that put him on the train for Holland. That, and the knowledge that his American royalties – quite good again, and the tourist articles had been reprinted over there – lasted much better in Holland than in Paris.

He found Elsa sitting alone, smoking a cigarette and brushing her hair. Her eyes looked tired; she seemed older and thicker, as though she had been drinking too much. To him she was still the most beautiful woman there was.

'Oh, Martin, I am so pleased to see you.' She talked furiously. What had he done? Where had he been? What were the plans? He basked in this welcome and this unaccustomed interest. This was not a raw English Miss, or a tousled Italian, smelling rather of sweat. His years of uprootedness were here crystallized into a centre.

'Have you any idea where I could find somewhere to live? I let the Emmastraat go. Too much rent, while I was away.'

'No, not really, though we can see. Town's packed; might be difficult. You can always stay here, if you like.'

'What about Erich? Won't he object?'

'He won't even notice. It's got that he's only here for bed and breakfast; it might be a *pension*, instead of his home.'

'And how's Mr MacPherson?' delicately.

'Poor Ken. He's gone; they didn't renew his contract. They would have ditched him earlier if they could. Poor darling; he didn't have great success here. He said that he couldn't learn to understand the Dutch mentality.'

Privately, Martin was not too terribly surprised.

'Not even yours?'

'Don't tease me Martin, I'm very miserable.'

'Strange how personal she has become,' he thought; 'so much less detached.'

She cheered up during the evening, and he went to the wine shop for a bottle of champagne, and they ate supper in a gay and careless mood of togetherness. She was genuinely pleased to see him back, that was clear. What was not clear? That he had been struck, sudden and devastating, with the *coup de foudre*. While she was making his bed in the spare room he said quietly, 'Wouldn't it be a good idea to go to bed together?'

She dropped an unfolded blanket and turned round without a word; came blind and helpless into his arms.

Making love to Elsa was disconcerting at first. That he had known her five years and never even touched her was unique in his experience. He was used to women that one kissed within the week, and after the third kiss one took their clothes off; it was well known. Strange too that at the age of thirty and with all her experience she had an odd ignorance, which he treated as innocence. It was as though she knew nothing about love; perhaps it was so. He had even to teach her how to reach her own sexual climax. And in the little arts of love she was shy and awkward.

The other thing to strike him was her abandon. She clutched love as the condemned man does hope; she clung to him like an exhausted swimmer, and her passion renewed itself like the hydra. As for him, he had a fury for her; he had the virility of a Bourbon and felt himself bewitched. Montespan, he thought; Athenais was like that. He became immensely possessive.

Things that had belonged to the unfortunate MacPherson – Penguin books, records, an old sweater, a strayed toothbrush – went mercilessly into the fire. All her old clothes were dumped in the dustbin. He told her to strip naked, and dressed her in new clothes from her skin up. He threw away her lipstick, her perfume. 'You begin from here,' he told her.

Their first year together was a flame that burned away all

his other interests. He planned his days round her. It was his rage that he could not sleep with her; he had to leave her at night, in her own bed, to wait for Erich, who would come in any moment humming '*Ah fuyez douce image*' with a gentle perfume of gin and cigars, and a head full of heaven knew what.

Other barriers imposed rules of conduct; her children for example. They saw and heard; they were *de trop*. Elsa could not risk an open breach with her husband, not while they were there. To Erich also they formed an effective bond with his wife; they made his home. He loved them dearly, took them out, followed their school work, bought their shoes, read to them. He might, certainly, be out till one in the morning; he might, equally, be home at half past five, to talk and play and work with them. These things cannot be swept aside.

Martin's behaviour was the more illogical. It seemed not to occur to him that this type of life was a poor enough expedient. He acted as though there would never again be anyone in his life but Elsa; he bound himself to her with every tie he could. While he roared about during this time, being as Bohemian as he could, any adult could have seen what he needed. Getting the opposite was a lot of fun but did not make him happy.

If Elsa was not there always, he made scenes. If she was late for an appointment, or failed in her share of some scheme, he suffered bitter pain. Looking for relief, he gnawed at his wounds. He indulged jealousies and little egotisms, and was often intensely disagreeable. She was patient and good-tempered, and encouraged the most preposterous ideas he could think up. He was trying to find his feet on a slippery slope; she rested on a summit of calm and fulfilment. 'My body feels so used,' she told him once. 'It does me so much good.'

He realized that it was impossible to stay in her house. He had still some fragments of independence. There, he could not breathe air that did not come from her lungs. He found a flat miles away by the Wester Park, and withdrew to his tent there. He was happy; unaware of himself, he was delightedly aware of her. He counted his joys well worth the torments.

He was immensely proud of her. Once, to a French friend in Amsterdam for a few days, he introduced her openly as his mistress, nor did she object. He told her he would like to put a man outside the flat, carrying a sandwich board with 'Elsa de Charmoy is my mistress' and his signature. He showed open possession everywhere, not caring who might see and comment. He would take her to shops and watch her try on, making coarse remarks ('I can't wait to get that off!') in front of shopgirls. He felt a need to be cruel, almost sadistic, to humiliate her. Sometimes, to this end, he did risky and outrageous things. The auto was his instrument in one of these.

His earnings came and went without his noticing or caring; with the impudence of immaturity he hated to dirty his hands with money. With one unusually large cheque he bought the auto, an Opel Kapitan, almost new. It became his pride, and a potent instrument of pleasure. In the evenings they might ride out to Aerdenhout or Bloemendaal. Coming back from such an evening, a day that Erich, bless him, had gone to Scheveningen for a chess tournament, they had allowed themselves to be very late; it was perhaps two in the morning when he stopped the car on the downs and said, 'Take off all your clothes.' He rode home without allowing her to dress. There were no lights on in the Matthew Marisstraat; in Amsterdam few people keep late hours. He handed her the door-key.

'Jump out and open the door.'

'But darling, the neighbours; I am naked.'

'There isn't a soul to be seen. I want to see you walk through the street. Naked. Just like that.'

She walked obediently and with dignity up to the door.

He was not able to say, afterwards, when things began to change. Some time when they had been lovers a year or more. It was too gradual to date with any certainty. The first episode was, maybe, his decision to go to France, after a year uninterruptedly together. He did not stay long; after ten days, in fact, his longing for her became uncontrollable. But when he came happily back, with several expensive presents, she made a scene.

'How many women did you sleep with?'

'Don't be a fool, Elsa, I beg you.'

'Catherine was not warm and welcoming?'

'I didn't see Catherine.'

'Imagine, now, that I would believe that!'

'I saw Max in the office and had lunch with him, and I believe that I totally forgot even to ask after her. Why choose to spoil the day I come home?'

'I don't mind being your mistress, but I do mind being an old sweater that you put on when you're cold.'

'You are making yourself ridiculous, do you realize?'

Martin never knew what this was all about; guessed later that perhaps he had shown an unexpected and unwanted independence in choosing suddenly to go to Paris at all. It was from this time that he dated their beginning to go down the hill. She reversed their roles, became herself possessive. She did this better than he did. There were no more scenes, but a campaign designed to tie him, physically, still more firmly to her. She had never objected to his little ferocities – now she began to encourage them.

The sequel to their row came two days later. He had not seen her, and walked in as though nothing had happened. She was tense and tearful.

'Do you sometimes think me a foul bitch? I don't know why I was so horrible, but I missed you so. Do you want to punish me?'

'Upon my word I do. I was very hurt. I broke my stay to come back quicker and I brought heaps of things. You weren't exactly welcoming.'

It was then that she produced the little riding switch.

'Beat me then; I want you to. Take my knickers down and beat me.'

He did, too.

The second episode was both vaguer and more complex. A man turned up one day at the Matthew Maris, with an introduction to Martin from an acquaintance in Paris. He was a Peruvian, doing some sort of business with a Dutch firm in Lima, and had to make some lengthy negotiation with the Chamber of Commerce in Amsterdam. Martin was not there that day, was not even there the whole week. He was busy with a new novel about the docks, and spent most of his day around the harbour. He was, in fact, working; the first time in a considerable while. Elsa made no effort to get hold of him; the gentleman from Lima was quite happy in her company. When Martin did come, tired and serene, Marcos had left that morning on a Rio plane from Schiphol.

It did not mean much at the time, except that he was rather indignant.

'But you didn't phone – the shop below will take messages; you know that.'

'But, darling, it wasn't sufficiently important. The man came only with a vague introduction, hoping to find someone who would take him about and entertain him a bit. You would have been very bored, and furious at being dragged away from the docks for a man from Lima. He had a straw hat with a coloured band, which he said were the Peruvian national colours; now I ask you! A ridiculous person; I was polite, seeing it was a friend of a friend of yours, and he amused me faintly, but that's nothing to get indignant about.'

Martin had to be satisfied with this explanation.

Whenever he felt that there was something a tiny bit fishy about one of Elsa's stories, he could be sure that then she was at her most reasonable and plausible. He was nearly ready to believe her, till letters began arriving, almost weekly, with a Lima postmark, in emotional typing passionately corrected with red ink. This too would, ordinarily, have amused him; indeed it did, till he saw that Elsa was encouraging this nonsense and writing in return, heaven only knew what.

'Lima is a white town, Spanish as Sevilla, very high above the sea among noble mountains. I can see you here, fair among fair houses. Roses bloom here as in the Caucasus; petals shower down upon flagstones till there exists an entire carpet of beauty that lasts but an hour – unlike yours – and must be constantly renewed. No music will be needed – the stillness will suffice, and the notes of the water, falling from the high fountains. A little wind rustles the tamarisks. I will lay you tenderly down among those rose-petals, and dark naked Indian girls will bring grapes and nectarines, for their naked blonde queen.'

'Do not the fireworks produce a magical effect, my naked blonde queen?' said Martin viciously. Elsa was indignant at his having found a letter she had thought well hidden, in a dull book – *Geschiedenis der Nederlandse Letterkunde*.

'Do you perhaps visualize dark gleaming Indian bodies when you are in bed with me?'

'It means nothing,' said Elsa calmly. 'It's pure fantasy, and with someone in South America you must admit that's pretty harmless.'

'In that case why hide the letters?'

'Don't think now that Erich would be best pleased. He can be odd. Total strangers writing embarrassing letters is just what might annoy him. We can't afford that in our position, you and I.' Clever defence.

'Did you sleep with this geyser while he was here?'

'You know adequately, I think, that I sleep with no one but you.'

The finale of this ridiculous incident came six months afterwards, when Martin was again living in the Matthew Maris. Elsa was out, having gone into the town to the dentist, and to talk to her German friend from the porcelain factory; she was in full flood of enthusiasm for this business. She came back with a high colour, and in that state of extreme calm that he knew meant excitement.

'You take a lot of trouble to impress your dentist.'

She was wearing her best clothes, a suit that had cost fifty pounds, bought, like every stitch she had, by Martin.

'To impress Willy Munch, you mean. He's not too convinced the figurines will sell.'

Her hair had been rather carelessly combed, and was falling down. 'Put your hair back.' He was behind her, and leaned forward to kiss her neck. She shook her head angrily; she no longer encouraged him. 'Your hair smells of Cuban tobacco.'

'Nonsense, that's that Macedonian stuff Willy Munch smokes. I was with him in the Stedelijk Museum, and afterwards coffee in Polen.'

These stories could not be shaken without making a fool of himself. He dropped the subject, hopelessly. For confirmation of his idea – that she looked as though she had made love – he had to wait three years, when it came out that she had told Sophia, as being a huge joke, that she had made love that day with Marcos, who was in Amsterdam on business, in his hotel room. He beat her, but it made him feel worse.

There were good days all the same during this time. Even happy days, when he remembered and recaptured something of their old camaraderie behind elaborate fantasies of sex. The night he drove down on to the beach in Zandvoort in the auto – a thing absolutely forbidden – in the middle of winter, and they made love in the sand half way to Noordwijk. On the way back a policeman caught them, and Martin gibbered in French and then explained, in bad German, that in France it was not done to pay attention to notices forbidding things. The day when out of sentiment they went to Apeldoorn – and made love in pinewoods, on a steep little hillside horribly slippery with needles, unable to stop themselves laughing. He told her that day about his ideas in the apple orchard, years before.

'You know, if you'd just grabbed me there and then I should have been very happy.'

Little things, to set against the slowly banking heap of memories gone sour and corrupt. The habit of her was eating him up, and only faint fibres of him showed still, as in a skeleton leaf. He left his flat, and came to live with her again, because a disconcerting thing happened unexpectedly. Erich van Kampen, good quiet man, had had enough of it.

He had perhaps observed the whole comedy with a sharper eye than anyone had given him credit for. He knew his wife, and gin had not impaired his judgment. Conceivably, he thought that there was simply no point in trying to put a face on a hopeless marriage when the harm done the children was greater than that done by an open break. His long standing technique of simply being passive was a good one, but he may have got sick of it in the end. Perhaps he would have done it long before if gin had not undermined determination. Was he finally repelled past endurance?

He quietly organized himself another job, in The Hague, an institute of prehistoric research with a resounding title, and arranged everything with care. When he was quite ready, and without having said a word beforehand, he calmly told Elsa that he was going, that he was taking the children, that he was also taking such furniture and household articles as he wanted, that the rent was paid till the end of the month, that she could do as she pleased but that he would – that day – be gone. The removers would be arriving at ten-fifteen, he did not intend to enter into any argument whatsoever, and was hers very sincerely. Whatever could be said about him, his handling of this situation was masterly.

Martin was in bed when there came a rapping on the door. Elsa did not say much, but that she had left her husband and was now his for ever. He got out of bed, gave her a drink – she was all white and shaky, most dramatic – and told her to get into bed and get warm. Quite a while later he thought of asking about the Matthew Maris. She could tell more of the truth by then, knowing he would not abandon her.

'But I can't stay there by myself.'

'I'll come with you and help with the rent. We can't afford to let it go, and it's a far better flat than this hole.'

A day later Martin's books, clothes, and typewriter had

neatly filled the gap left by Erich, who had in the end taken scarcely anything beyond personal oddments of just that sort.

Martin sold the auto; it was becoming too much of a luxury. He was not earning, and he had now to carry the household in earnest, paying food, light and coal bills. He was doing no work. His harbour book had got stranded on a mudbank half-way through, and he had done nothing since. He slipped, during these months, into a comatose indifference to everything; he did not even answer letters from his publisher asking what the hell he thought he was doing. He disregarded the world. He read a great deal, played endless records, wrote bits of plays, bits of filmscripts, short stories, began – lackadaisically – to collect material for a study of Ibsen. 'I am Peer Gynt,' he said frequently. He said he had to learn Norwegian. 'The translations are all tripe.' Elsa brooded for a week before coming to her own decision.

'I am going to find work. I have wasted the best years of my life as a housewife here; I want now to do something real.' It was typical of her that she should have seen anything unreal in being a housewife.

She got into a habit quickly of being out all day.

'Stay in this stinking hole, where I have sat indoors for ten years, never going out, watching the baker on his tricycle, gossiping with the milkman, pah!' An absolute frenzy developed of hunting up dear old friends, unseen since the Mac-Pherson days, and sometimes since long before, mysterious figures of her *louche* period, unknown to Martin.

How she came to meet Herman Ketelboer he had no idea. But she came home happy, filled with a springtime of joy and life he had not seen since their first days together. He did not put this down to a lover, despite his biting jealousy; it was an intellectual excitement, for once.

'I have found something I think I can do.' She was in a characteristic attitude, sitting on her heels with her outdoor coat still on. 'I said quite absently to Herman that I wished I could do somehing with my hands. He has very clever hands

93

himself – he's an amazing pianist by the way. He had a most interesting idea. He says I should do sculpture, that is to say modelling, really.'

Martin was rather cross that other people told her what to do, especially an idea he had not had himself, and that she should listen submissively – even worse!

'Extraordinary idea.'

'Not the least extraordinary' – she was nettled. 'I know that it is so. I can feel things with my hands – forms, contours – I know perfectly well I could do it.'

'What sort of things? People, or animals, or abstractions, or what? Do you just want to make china bulls, or do you wish to invent? It's not a very easy technique, I don't think. It's easy to say one has a talent for modelling – indeed I think you have – but you need surely a good deal of training and practice before you can handle the material with any kind of freedom. You could be primitive, perhaps. Bulls from Lascaux caves; naïve figures of gorillas – Douanier Rousseau.'

'I thought about all that; I discussed it too with Herman. He knows someone who is a sculptor, and gave me an introduction. I'm to go and see her this evening. It's a Madame Pauline Ter Laan, and she lives in Haarlem. Herman has treated her for arthritis. She's about sixty now, he says, and doesn't work any more, but she was well known before the war, and exhibited regularly in Paris. He thinks she'll teach me, if I've any talent.'

Martin was really very pleased, on reflection. The idea made him proud and happy, as though Elsa's possession of some other talent conferred an obscure dignity upon himself. Her enthusiasm that night was even greater.

'Darling, she was so nice. It's a very pleasant house, one of those big old-fashioned places in the Frederikspark, full of ridiculous things and wonderful enormous furniture. Her husband was a doctor in Indonesia; there are lots of Javanese and Balinese things – he raises orchids for a hobby, he's about seventy now. She has five children – one is a doctor too – but the only one I saw was the youngest girl, who still lives at home. About twenty-five I suppose, pretty – not your type though –'

'Look, take breath.'

'Am I gibbering? Well, she took me inside and made coffee, and then Madame came in, tall, rather splendid looking, like Sarah Bernhardt, with a lovely voice. She said it was as Herman had thought, that she did not work seriously any longer, but that if I were interested she would show me the elementary techniques, not formal lessons but that she'd help. She has a studio full of stuff which I saw; some very striking things. You would be interested in the house, and in her too; fascinating person. Not a bit old; on the contrary.'

Martin felt rather bored, and did not really have much enthusiasm for this artistic ménage, but said dutifully, 'Does the husband still practise?'

'Yes, I think so, but not strenuously I imagine. Ear, nose and throat.'

'And what are you thinking of? Going there and having lessons, then? Try this idea out in detail?'

'Yes; I could go every day, couldn't I? I do want to make a real effort.'

'I haven't yet got a very precise idea of what you want to make of it. Something serious? You would like to try and become professional?'

'Yes, if I can.' She thought a while and added, 'I do so want to do something decisive, something vigorous.'

He was happier with Elsa at work, and these days of decision and vigour infected him to some purpose. He made a determined effort and finished his harbour book, and took it himself to Paris to his publisher.

This gentleman was called Monsieur Jouhandeau. He overcame the disadvantages of this ridiculous name by being very businesslike, and by a youthful appearance. He was a smartly dressed, elegant man who was clever behind a flippant façade.

'Good God, I thought you were dead.'

'I've been ill.'

'You don't look any too well and that's a fact. Pale like a dead fish's belly. Have you got something for me?'

'Yes. Book length. Left it with your secretary.'

'Now that's good. At last. You have a nerve, not answering my letters!'

'I tell you, I've been ill.'

'Ill! I know these illnesses. Have them myself sometimes. Never mind; if the book's any good I'll forgive you. Do you realize you've done nothing for two years? That English joke was all very well – it did quite good business here oddly enough – but it's all a bit light weight, all that. Time you grew up – began to communicate more important experiences than English suburban bedrooms and tea-tables.'

'This is just the thing for you,' grinned Martin. 'It's serious, all about a girl who works in a harbour brothel.'

'Oh God, like Dédé d'Anvers. Never mind, perhaps it will make a filmscript. That brothel stuff is not much good for America, my boy, and that's where the sales make money. And our New York agent wants more from you, lots more. What did he get? – those piddling holiday things. We haven't that many authors who translate well, and we have to keep the flag flying. Good strong satirical stuff. You know,' with an indulgent, wicked smile, 'something cynical. Americans think Europe so cynical. You should see Simenon's sales over there; cunning, very cunning.

'I wish you'd go to Tahiti or somewhere – this damned woman you've got there in Holland is gnawing away your guts, I do believe. Now don't make indignant faces; come on, we're going to have lunch together. You look as though you need plenty to drink and a damned good meal. Bloody miserable, in fact. I wish you'd get shot of this awful woman; I'm convinced she stultifies you.'

'You don't know her, and you won't get the chance to, either.'

'I knew it, all cuddly and maternal. Don't want to know her, hate her guts quite enough as it is. Claire, put that manuscript in my briefcase and see that I take it home tonight. If there's anything really important, I'm going to La Méditerranée; we might meet Ludwig Bemelmans, who knows?

'How do you like my new car? I've gone old and grey waiting for a new model from Citroen though there's all sorts of exciting gossip about one, so I got this Lancia – the girls simply love it. Lively, isn't she? Tiny bit rough, I find, but the acceleration – like this – in second gear – boum – that's what you need here, something that leaves the other bastard with fallen arches.

'Now, we're going to have the very devil of a lunch; enormous steak with great quantity of marrow; damn these black-and-white cows of yours; Charolais is what you need. Paul, two Fernet Brancas and a table – a nice table, not that penal colony of yours down the step. And we want oily food, nothing with butter, that's most important; you don't know my friend, he comes from Holland, so no butter, Paul, you realize? *Aioli, bouillabaisse, langoustes,* not for me, I loathe all that Provençal muck. *Rouget,* that's it, *rouget* in little paper bags.'

'Yes,' said Martin happily.

'Now,' said Jouhandeau pleasantly, after an enormous meal and a good deal to drink, 'why don't you go to Hyères or Porquerolles, and get a bit of colour, and after a month the garlic will have got the worms out of your system and your head will be full of fresh ideas. Come back then to me – if you're short I'll advance you some money – and we'll have a long serious conversation. We'll know if this brothel stuff of yours is any good. Sounds to me as though you've been living too long in brothels. I've nothing against them at the right time, but living in them is apt to be a very destructive experience. Why the devil you can't come and live here where you belong escapes me – never mind that, Porquerolles is the place for you, and a good gutty Italian girl of sixteen.'

Nevertheless he went straight back to the Matthew Maris.

He would have very much liked to go to Porquerolles; it was a thoroughly attractive idea as well as a good one. But he was not only tied strongly to Elsa by an old passion; he had also an obscure sense of duty towards her. She lived entirely on his earnings, since she hadn't a penny. He was propped up by these two things; the sense of obligation towards her, and the muddled notion that when one loved truly it must come all right in the end. He knew that she understood him, and thought that he understood her. Bound by circumstances as well as by loyalty they could surely overcome the wear and tear of emotional upheavals.

There might have been some truth in this if he had assessed her character correctly; his mistake was in attributing to her his own generous motives. He should have gone to Porquerolles shrugging, saying, 'Ah she'll find another friend to keep her warm, and if not – well there is always the Reeperbahn.' But he was not that kind of person. As her oldest friend and her lover he felt deeply indebted and involved, and compelled by loyalty.

The physical bond between them was no longer so strong. He was unaccustomed to the fact that in love familiarity breeds boredom, especially when you are not married. Now that he could watch her, for instance, washing – or turn over lazily in bed and reach out to touch her whenever he wished – he became perfunctory as a lover – a thing, rather, that he did because it was expected of him. Sitting in the train, he did not think of these self-evident facts.

Often, very often in later years, he would wonder about his state of mind during this time. Why was it that with some experience as a writer, and a knowledge of the world fairly considerable for twenty-seven years, he had failed so utterly to turn his experience to any use in his own surroundings? He could never give an adequate answer; he thought later that he had simply lacked elementary common sense. Witch she might be – had he really walked all those years in so deep an enchanted sleep, with so little idea how to handle and shape his own emotions? Had he really been just very immature? Certainly nothing of this permeated to his consciousness as he sat in the train, watching the landscape of Holland flash past. He was just happy, in a doggy way.

He walked from the station instead of taking the tram. Down the Leidsestraat he breathed in delightedly – the smell of Amsterdam is enchanting. He was in a thoroughly good humour when he opened the flat door in the Matthew Maris. In the living-room a girl was sitting, who got up, a little unsure of herself. He was as startled as she was.

'I'm sorry,' he said automatically.

She stood still, holding the book she had been reading. 'I came in with Mrs de Charmoy; she went out but she said she would not be long.' She held out her hand. 'Sophia Ter Laan.'

He introduced himself. 'I've heard about you, but only just, I'm afraid.'

'I've heard about you,' she said, smiling.

'Nothing horrible I hope?'

'Why should I have heard anything horrible?'

He grinned. 'It was only a conventional remark. Please sit down again; I'm very happy to meet you.'

While they made conversation he studied her. As Elsa had said, she was about twenty-five; quiet and gentle in her movements. Tall; taller and slimmer than Elsa, but durable and well put together. Her body was too big in the bones for a dancer's, but she had all a dancer's suppleness. Her hair was a funny colour, not brown, but a gold so deep as to have bronze shadows and honey-coloured highlights. Her brows were long and unusually straight; her eyes had a slant upwards at the outside corners. She had a thin, high-boned face, full of quiet, with the dark, almost Indian colour one sees by the sea in Holland – a smuggler's colour that is more than just sun tan. Her eyes had no grey in them but were a surprising deep blue, true as a sapphire. She needed severe dressing, and wore with credit a plain black skirt and sweater. Her hands were large and very well shaped.

'Did you say that Elsa was long gone?'

'I think she's only doing some shopping.'

'Because I was going to suggest your staying for dinner.'

'Thank you very much, but I know you'd prefer to be alone with her.'

'Know?' Martin lifted his eyebrows.

'It's not especially a secret, is it? Please don't think me rude but perhaps I'd better not wait for her; I must really take myself off.'

'I don't think you in the least rude, but I'll be upset if you go. Please have a cigarette and I'll try and find something for us to drink.'

She did not quarrel, and sat down with self-possession.

'I want to know more about you. I only know that your mother's been very kind to Elsa.'

'My mother enjoys it very much. So do we all. Elsa is wonderful company.'

'Do you keep house for your mother?'

'Not especially. I help her. Do I look as though I should be a housewife?' The question was serious, and altogether without archness.

'I don't know what you should be,' said Martin, surprising himself, 'but I'm quite convinced you're good at it.'

She laughed. 'I am good at housekeeping too, but I hate it.'

They had stopped chatting and begun talking when the outside door banged, and Elsa was smiling at him with her arms full of parcels; her complicated, calculated smile. She looked fresh and rested, and very pretty; damp evening air had made her sparkle and tightened the wave in her hair, making the skin of her face look new and young.

'Hallo, darling,' her voice was deep and affectionate. 'Why didn't you let us know – never mind, there's plenty for supper. You've met Sophia then. We've been in the Kalverstraat. Did they accept your book?'

'François took it with him; I'll hear nothing for a week or so.'

'Have you been telling terrible things to Sophia? Has he amused you, or just been tiresome?'

'I have been enjoying myself very much' – her voice was even deeper than Elsa's – 'but you know I really must go home.'

'She is a very pleasant, agreeable sort of a girl,' said Elsa at the closed door, 'but stupid as a cow.'

This was the first of many conversations with Sophia. He did not find her in the least stupid. She took no pains to be attractive. No archness, whimsy, hair-tossing. She was utterly un-flirtatious. He could talk to her without fear of having a word repeated; a valuable attribute. She had a history degree from the University of Paris, but was not sentimental about either her education or the Sorbonne.

'Live in Paris and study history, and both ways you learn philosophy.'

She had an unwillingness to trust herself, a refusal to con-fide. She upset people by a sharp tongue and an open scepticism about the honesty of anyone. Her immense capacity for silence made many take her for a stupid person. She was quite uninterested in her mother's art, and lukewarm indeed about all arts, which scandalised Martin, who lectured her, at length, about mental laziness. Elsa did nothing to discourage his seeing her, and even asked Sophia to go over and spend the evening in the Matthew Maris when she herself was in Haarlem. The idea was possibly to distract him; she certainly did not regard Sophia as a rival.

Martin got to like her, and she, very slowly, to trust him. She was a lonely and discontented girl who did not know what she wanted from life. Her mother found her frankly tiresome, and said so.

'I don't know if it's a husband you want; you certainly aren't going a very clever way about it. You don't make friends because you won't mix with people your own age. Then you make a friend of someone rather unsuitable, I can't help feel-ing. You are all day over there in Amsterdam. That man is by

101

all accounts very neurotic, and is besides deeply involved with Elsa. I'm very fond of Elsa, thoroughly intelligent and delightful girl, but she seems to have lived a rackety life, and I cannot believe that this man's ideas and opinions will be of great value.'

'The trouble with Mother,' said Sophia, telling Martin about this, 'is that she is unnecessarily puritanical. She had a hard life, and tends to believe that having a beastly time when young is in itself virtuous. We should be starving for our art, whatever it is. She does not really trust your being successful. You ought to be making a precarious living at something sober and getting up at four in the morning for art. And I should be being useful as a doctor or a missionary or something. I hate offices; I hate housekeeping. I had a year in England as a mother's help to learn English, and another in Austria for German; I loathed every minute of it. Why should I be a secretary or a plane stewardess? My father loves me dreadfully because in his eyes I am still his baby daughter; he shakes his head and talks to his flowers; I've heard the muttering. Something like: "She's a child and doesn't know what she wants. But she has no fun. She should join the operetta club, go skating and swimming, meet more young men. She needs amusing, ought to have gaiety and companionship. She sits at home listening to the radio, smoking herself to death and reading trashy books; what's wrong with her?" '

Martin laughed; he was getting this girl to come gradually out of her shell. Elsa and Mrs Ter Laan had gone to a party, to which neither he nor Sophia had been invited. He had been the more content to find that Sophia detested parties as much as he did. They had decided to have a little party of their own, and had a wild duck with raw mushrooms, and a bottle of Corton Charlemagne. Sophia was wearing tight grey trousers and a white shirt, lying on her back on the floor. Martin, who had eaten too much, was smoking a huge cigar. They were both enjoying themselves.

She put tango records on the gramophone, and did a fake

Balinese dance, graceful and ridiculous. Later, they had a long silly argument. When you crossed the Pont des Arts, headed towards the Luxembourg, was that the Rue de Seine or the Rue Bonaparte?

'Would you like to live in Paris?'

'No; I loved it as student, but not to live, I think, not without pots and pots of money, and have a house with a garden. No gardens in Paris. What about you?'

'To be honest, I prefer being here.'

'You don't belong here; in this house, I mean. As a tame pussy, you do not altogether fit.'

She had said too much, and swerved away from the subject. When she took away his ashtray – she disliked dirty ashtrays – he took her hand and sat her on his lap, where she stayed bolt upright.

'You'll soon get sick of that; I'm heavier than I look.'

'Don't talk so much,' kissing her. She responded to the kiss politely, even generously, and got up promptly.

'I'm sorry but I was not particularly comfortable. And you would only get fancy ideas about taking my clothes off.'

'Didn't have any ideas.'

'Everybody has ideas,' placidly. 'I am an exceedingly cold woman, I got told so twenty times a day in Paris, and was poorly regarded on that account. Even here everyone notices; it is why I have few friends; I am discouraging, and aware of the fact.'

'I am not particularly discouraged.'

'Isn't it rather bad manners to kiss me in your mistress's house?'

'My house; I pay the rent.'

'Not the point; I expressed myself badly. Put it that I do not very much approve of being kissed in a house where you maintain another woman. She's a friend of mine too.'

'Apart from that, do you mind my kissing you?'

'I like it,' with gravity. 'Anyway, my dear, you shouldn't be paying the rent. I hope you get your money's worth.'

103

'I'm not always too sure of that either,' he said, rather ruefully.

It was a month or two later, with a cold wet autumn sliding into a cold wet winter, that Martin, who had been caught out and drenched without an overcoat and then had to wait half an hour for a bus, got a touch of 'flu. He stayed in, wound in sweaters, drinking cognac and eating codeines. When he put a pen to a sheet of paper his handwriting was clumsy and childish; unnerving.

'I feel full of 'flu,' he told Elsa.

'Poor darling; that's rotten. I hope I don't catch it all the same; I badly want to stay clear-headed just now. In a way you're to blame, though; you don't get enough fresh air, and when you do go out you overdo it and take silly risks.'

'I'm going to make my bed up in the other room. I'll probably be restless and plunge about a great deal.'

'Yes, that's a good idea. I'm sorry to sound unsympathetic, but I'm trying to persuade those people at the *fabriek* to paint and glaze a figure for me. They aren't interested of course; bloody Dutch. Ten thousand hideous delft windmills a year. Mrs Ter Laan has thought of some people in Germany who might help . . .' She was gone, after an agonized hunt for a pair of stockings without ladders.

Martin sat by the stove, feeling ghastly. When the buzzer went, and he heard Sophia's voice on the speakbox, he felt like a shipwrecked sailor seeing the posse arrive – he was at the point where one does not care how badly the metaphors get mixed.

She came in happily, but looked concerned when she took a look at him.

'Hey, hey; what's up with you?'

'I just don't feel too gay. 'Flu pains. Just a bad cold, I think.'

'Nonsense, I'm going to look at you. You certainly have 'flu my boy; you're a vile sight – why aren't you in bed?'

'Bed nothing – except with you, perhaps.'

'You reassure me. Ill, but evidently not all that ill. First bed. I take it you sleep with Elsa?'

'No, I'm sleeping in the other room.'

Sophia surveyed the bedroom with the sarcastic smile he knew; virgin faced with adultery. With professional, rather brutal hands she undressed and pushed him into bed.

'Too superior to wear pyjamas, I see. Pity I haven't a pair of mine by me. Now stay quiet. Is there a thermometer anywhere in this house? Of course not; we'll see first about making you comfortable. I can see you've a temperature; how high it is doesn't matter much.'

He submitted with the passive enjoyment of all men who feel a little ill, imagine they are dying, and like to have a loving, fussing woman preside at the deathbed.

'I must say I don't like the sound of your breathing a bit. Lie flat; I'm going to listen to you.'

'Can you tell?' He watched the absorbed face with one ear laid against his bare chest, and felt affection as well as desire.

'I'm a doctor's child; we used to do this when we were small. You've pleurisy, my boy. Not very serious I judge, but I'll have to go home and get some things; I'll be back early this afternoon. Now you're going to drink very hot tea with lemon, and tonight I'll make *soupe au vin*.'

She took his keys and left him feeling low; he got much lower before she came back with a shopping bag.

'Ha! Feel awful? Good; I'll resurrect the corpse. First off, good old penicillin; not allergic?'

'No.'

'Had any recently enough to be resistant?'

'Yah.'

'Next, a drink. Wasn't a student in France for nothing. This is a speciality. Orangeflower, *verveine, anis* and *tilleul,* and you're going to get buckets of it. Now – hupsake!' – holding up the syringe and squinting for the air-bubble – 'intramuscular; heavens, there's nothing to get hold of in this tiny little behind of yours ... I'm going to stay all night, all virtue. I'll

105

sleep with Elsa, ha ha! She's delighted at not having the responsibility of looking after you; I'm beginning to take a dislike to that woman. Boo, your temperature is quite high, over thirty-six that's not unusual with any congestion of the lung. Your *tisane* is ready; drink it as hot as you can manage ... My poor dear you're very feverish. Try and get all the sleep you can; I'm going to do a bit of shopping and tidy up; living-room's a pigsty.'

If there was a definite moment at which he began to love her that was probably it. Shut in the spare room he listened intently to the small sounds of the house; her footsteps, the clink of china, the whine of the cleaner, the hiss and rumble of the lavatory plug. Fragments of song drifted from the kitchen as he fell asleep. Love had become a string of French flowers – orange, *anis, tilleul, verveine* – Sophia. Like a litany. She was singing the Schubert melody, *'Alle Seelen ruhn in Frieden,'* he said to himself, nine-tenths asleep.

She was not at all forthcoming. As a nurse, excellent, knowing exactly when he wanted food and bringing it, knowing how to make his bed comfortable, forcing him to shave, sitting the afternoon long by him silently knitting. 'Would you like the gramophone? What shall I put on?' He was delighted that she close his favourite Stravinsky symphonies, and disillusioned to find that she had barely known the composer's name.

'I'd seen a photograph of him somewhere – wonderful looking man; I thought I'd like the music.' Women's reasoning.

'And did you?'

'Fairly well. I never really like anything passionately the first time.'

But she was tart. After two days of fever he began to get convalescent, and mildly sexy with it, in a frivolous way. He was stupid enough to pat her bottom. She did not react except to move away, but his next injection was disagreeable.

'Certainly. I took a blunt needle and stabbed in nice and heavy. Take liberties with my buttocks, watch your own, buster. When you're better, which will not take long, you can have a nice orgy with Elsa.'

'Spiteful!'

'We have long conversations, by no means all about you, don't flatter yourself.'

'Awful intimate feminine confidences.'

'Don't imagine ever that I confide in other women; disgusting.'

Elsa he scarcely saw; she put her nose in two or three times to radiate hearty goodwill for a few minutes. With Sophia doing the housekeeping she was away happily all day, and when she did come back was withdrawn and thoughtful. Nor, when he was well enough to move back into her bed, was she very enthusiastic. She grumbled a good deal about having to make love, with rather an air of doing it for therapeutic value.

Concerning himself and Sophia she had thought up a masterly technique. Basically: the adults have at the moment no time for games, but we are all so pleased to see the children good together and not worrying us. She was always very fluent, he knew from Sophia, with Mrs Ter Laan in the studio, full of philosophical profundities.

'Makes me sick to listen to the foolishness. Very much of it is about how patient and long-suffering she is with you. Hopelessly nervous and unstable, half alcoholic, quite unable to live at all without her guiding hand and deep, loving knowledge of your little ways. Nothing, in short, but her good advice and stabilizing influence keeps you from being totally derailed. Mother of course tut-tuts, and probably ripostes, when I'm safely gone, with tales of what a difficult child I was and am.

'Then there's the husband stuff. Deserted by the drunken and dissolute man who ran away to The Hague. She's practically the little match girl. Trying to turn her talent into enough commercial success to buy her bread. No mention made of either your talents or your ability to earn your living, and that makes me mad. I know I'm being unlike my sweet self, but she's so uncaring and ungrateful. As though she'd ever be short of someone to keep a roof over her.'

'My dear, you are peevish.' Martin did not really believe very much of this. He had concluded that – without perhaps realizing – Sophia was jealous.

She was not going to respond to any little tricks, still less any effort to seduce her, since if she was over half in love herself she would be damned if she would play second fiddle to Elsa, to be taken to bed when madam was in a bad mood, or had the curse. Martin had begun to seesaw, and found it a disagreeable sensation.

Intellectually he was coming in a dim way to realize that a life with Elsa was not a permanency either desirable or even very likely. He had not come to any logical conclusion; his emotions were still his master, and he could not make a decision. He sensed a new, strong attraction to a younger, better-looking woman, with a more upright and more sympathetic character. Freshness, innocence, and unselfishness, instead of the tired, stale flesh of a woman in middle age who had never made a success of any of her relationships with men. That was how he felt when Elsa was away.

When she came back he would recover his loyalty and his sense of indebtedness. Both were reinforced by her incomparable seduction. He would then wonder what on earth he saw in a green and prim little girl, who was certainly very nice – intelligent, kind and gay – but how could she possibly compare? Ridiculous to call Elsa middle-aged: she was under thirty-five, at her best, with perhaps no longer the supple slimness of youth, but in the full brilliance of unusual beauty and unparalleled seductiveness. The perfect mistress, with the intelligence and wit that make the good courtesan incomparable company. Marguerite de Valois, Léa de Lonval – Madame de. Not a La Vallière, nor even a Montespan, nor, really *'sincère et tendre Pompadour'*. But very decidedly what Sir Charles Mendl would have called a ravishing creature. History had always been adorned by such women. Delighted with this masterpiece of self-deception, Martin launched into an Indian summer of love.

Sophia's absence made this easier. He had not stopped seeing her; the pot had suddenly boiled over, and put the fire out underneath. 'La Rochefoucauld,' he had been telling her, 'says that every woman is a science.'

'Are you collecting epigrams? If so I know a good one by John Donne.'

'Tell, then.'

> ' "Klockius hath so deeply sworn
> Ne'er more in bawdy house to come
> That he dare not go home." '

'Ow!'

'The literature of love teaches one some sharpish truths, or should,' said Sophia, and burst into tears. They had a classic thunderstorm, all the way from cold disdain and acid remarks to a lovely upheaval of emotional union. He rocked her in his arms and stroked her forehead.

'Oh my dear, my dear, I wish I could make you believe that I love you dearly.'

'Don't please claim that you love me; you are fond of me, I know, but the word love is not the key to my bedroom, nor an aspirin that you can keep me quiet with. Perhaps it keeps you quiet to tell yourself that you love me, but I don't believe it. You are caught in a dilemma and you cannot get loose, I think. I am so unhappy; I don't know whether I love you or not, but I hate to see you so bound. You have known her and loved her for eight years, and I've only known you eight weeks, but she is destroying you; it is true what she says. You are a wreck, every day more at war with yourself, less sure of your own ability to stand on your two feet. People who are wrecked by love are pathetic. If you had a job and weren't at home always it would be easier perhaps; the paypacket at the end of the month. You would have other loyalties, other obligations. Worries and little anxieties of *kleine leute*. You stay here in this horrible house eating yourself up, and your life has become complete fantasy, illustrated by sayings of La Rochefoucauld. I'm so angry with myself, that I can do nothing.'

The row did not solve anything; like most rows it was quite inconclusive. Martin did realize that she was more under his skin than he had known, and saved his conscience with the thought that he would not be seeing her any more. He was gentle and thoughtful towards Elsa, in an ostentatious way, but she gave no sign of having noticed.

Elsa wanted to go to Germany to visit the porcelain factory. She had had a letter; kind, flowery and businesslike.

'They are interested in any original work that might reproduce well but – oh, a long list of careful qualifications. The suggestion is that I call at the factory, bringing some pieces of work, when they will consider blah blah – darling, do you think that I could go?'

'What does Mrs Ter Laan think?'

'Doesn't really know, she says. It was an idea of hers; I did some of those little figures and she suggested they might suit the medium, but there are problems of which she knows nothing. The painting and glazing and so on. Then there's the question of either porcelain or faïence, and I want to pick these people's brains if I can, even if they don't accept anything, about the technical processes and the economics of it.'

'I suppose it wouldn't be more than four hours by train. You could go and bring back some nice sausage. I'm all for your going.'

'Just that you can't bear the idea of my being away a day.'

'Yes. Even a day. Do you know, I wonder, how much I love you?'

Elsa stroked his hair; she was sitting on the arm of his chair. 'What hurts me is that you love me, but find it so hard to trust me, when I know that I am much more trustworthy than lovable. We see love differently – I remember being so angry about Catherine, and it hurt me, though I knew that to you it was meaningless and that you loved me constantly. I don't let it come between us, even when you are slipping into bed with Sophia whenever you get the chance. As long as it is me you love. Where are you going this morning?'

'Reference library – Keizersgracht. Ibsenizing. Ring up the railways and try to work out how long the journey takes.'

'I don't think more than a day and a night. If I get there by lunch-time, I could probably take a train the following morning, or evening at the latest I suppose. Darling, one thing. Don't think I'd ever try to catch you out – come back suddenly or so. But if you're here with Sophia, don't take her into our bed, will you? That really would be an outrageous thing, which would injure me dreadfully. Please, please, for my sake.'

'Now why,' thought Martin, walking up towards the Keizersgracht, 'is she so certain that I go to bed with Sophia? Is she encouraging me, as cover for some naughty escapade of her own? What can be behind all that?'

Elsa went to Germany the next day. Martin did not see Sophia. Had some little hint been dropped to the girl? He found the situation obscure. He had misjudged Elsa, and Elsa had misjudged Sophia. Who was fooling who? He had not much objectivity.

He had not taken the row seriously. He was immunized to rows – with Elsa they followed a defined pattern of invective and things thrown – a flowerpot or a hotwater bottle, which had burst splendidly on impact – most satisfying. For Sophia's *Sinterklaas* present he had sent a beautiful and expensive present: a silk slip and camiknickers, midnight blue, embroidered with tiny silver stars and crescent moons. This was tactless, and he should not have been so outraged when the parcel was returned with a gentle note. 'They are very pretty and I am grateful, but you must realize that I cannot accept any presents from you.'

He was disappointed and angry, but said nothing and gave them to Elsa as though that had been the idea all along; she was delighted. This piece of hypocrisy was made ignoble when she asked, 'Aren't you giving Sophia anything for the Sint?'

'You are the woman I give presents to, my darling,' in a sanctified voice.

'Have you had a row with her?'

'No, but I haven't seen her for a while. She's very touchy; I trod on her toes in some way.'

Elsa had had quite a good reception in Germany.

'They were polite, and seemed impressed. They said that none of the things I had brought were really suitable, but that they showed talent. They said that they remained interested, and would consider with sympathy anything I submitted. A lot like that, and I should think perhaps of things with a tourist appeal, like the Dusseldorf Radschlager. The Germans are so vulgar. I've been trying to think; not little Hummel *mannetjes* of course, but something like the Copenhagen Little Mermaid. Think of something typically Dutch.'

'Badeloch and Gijsbrecht van Amstel.'

'Something tourists have heard of, stupid.'

'Portraits? You know, Doctor Plesman.'

'Not much good, I think. They tend to become parodies. Churchill on a beer mug. I want to avoid all that. They say that it's not worth putting a piece into production for a *luxe* market only; the costs are tremendous. I wonder –'

'What?'

'Whether I'll have to face the fact that I may never have enough talent to do real work. Remember Ginette, playing the piano in her night-club.'

She went daily still to Haarlem and worked steadily at the exercises Mrs Ter Laan set her to do. Certainly she was developing; she had more freedom and spirit in her handling of material. At home she modelled things that were interesting her at the time – Hindu gods with many arms, engaged in obscene activities, African woodwork, Gothic stone-carving, innumerable animals – to learn movement.

'I do get sick of gargoyles, and those old orang-outangs in the zoo.'

'Purifies the eye.'

'Suppose so; true that I'm ashamed already of those things I took to Germany.'

'There you are, you see.'

He noticed that she was coming under Herman's influence in many ways. She talked to him about art out of politeness of a sort; it was Herman's judgement upon which she acted. She went to see him often, and without trying to hide these visits, she was secretive and cagy about them.

'Herman's old woman has died,' she said suddenly one day over coffee.

'Old woman?'

'Who did the housekeeping.'

'Well, I'm sorry for him but sorrier for the old woman. How is it supposed to interest me?'

'It's that I hate it dreadfully that you support me; it's not right. As you know I took up this modelling with the idea of earning something if possible, as well as the self-respect of being able to use my hands to some purpose. But for a short term expedient I want to do some simple work; I could find the time. I couldn't work in an office, but this is only mornings; half receptionist and half cleaner. Bit of polishing and painting; cooking his dinner and keeping the appointment book and the accounts. He didn't think of this – it's entirely my idea – but I think he'd be sympathetic if asked since he knows I haven't a penny. I could help, anyway, then; I think it so unfair for you to have the whole burden of the household.'

He did not like the idea at all, but he gave in finally, when she kept begging him. It seemed selfish to refuse, and in truth, while he did not admit it, the money would help. When she came home with money that she had earned, proud as a seventeen-year-old, he was touched. And he was spending more than he should, up to the limit of his income.

Jouhandeau had not been enthusiastic about the harbour book; had said indeed roundly that it was tripe and sold it to a magazine specializing in tough serials, refusing to publish it himself; he said that it could do Martin's reputation no good. It did put money in the bank when badly needed. Everything had looked very poor; urged by Sophia he had done a series of 'I cover the waterfront' things and they had gone to the New York agent. He had done Hamburg, Copenhagen, Amsterdam, Rotterdam, Antwerp, Bordeaux, Marseilles and Genoa, which had with his earlier pieces been reprinted in book form and were now supporting him, uneasily.

'Baby talk,' Jouhandeau had written, disgustedly. It did not worry him very greatly that he was doing so little; he knew he was not written out, but undergoing a maturing process. It was accumulating inside him, and would come out when ready.

Elsa never showed anxiety now about his work, nor even curiosity, but in justice he always refused to discuss the subject, and became tetchy if she mentioned it. Sophia had said, direct as usual, that if one was caught in a psychological knot it was only logical to do one's best to get out of it. He had given this remark an indignant reception.

There was a New Year party on Herman's boat. It was a good idea; the boat was surprisingly big. Inside there was ten feet of headroom, much more than one imagined from the quayside. One entered through a companionway, down three steps into the kitchen, where there was always a good smell. Next to the kitchen was the room where patients waited and Herman had meals, and both read unlikely papers, so that one got housewives with the *Connoisseur* and predikants of the Reformed Church with the *News of the World*. A neatly painted notice said: 'If you have an appointment please buzz once and wait. If you have no appointment please buzz twice and wait. Consulting hours 10-12 and 2-4 by appointment only.' In this room there was a very beautiful crystal vase of very beautiful flowers; new ones were bought every day and Herman said that their therapeutic value was unbelievable.

A door from here led into the main room where Herman lived and worked – he slept in a cubby-hole at the front of the boat, and the bathroom was at the extreme back; total strangers had been known to use the lavatory. The big room was a long narrow oblong, floored with Chinese straw matting and severely furnished. Banquettes down the sides; bookshelves above and cupboards below. A big working table, an examination couch, a writing desk and an upright piano. No chairs. There was a porcelain stove and a coffee table; that was all. The woodwork was plain teak, unvarnished, and the seats were plain leather.

'He has some good jade and crystal but we put it away; no sense in risking anything good with a room full of people.' Elsa was shaking out her hair by the glass. Martin felt in good form; they were the first to arrive, since Elsa 'had to finish getting the food ready', and he had Herman to himself for half an hour. He drank Pernod and talked about Felix Kersten, Russian dancers, Balanchine, Hieronymus Bosch and Porsche cars. He knew little about any of these, but was a good brain-picker, knowing how to make people talk; they got on well and took a liking to each other.

The doctor was as tall as he was, rather broader, ten years older and a great deal better looking; evidently knew his job, and was both widely read and very intelligent. It should have been a good party. Elsa acted as hostess, which she did well; she was quite as good at conversation as he was. She seemed to know everyone, including half a dozen men he had never seen.

Why did Martin feel that he was not happy? Because Elsa was being rather the lady of the manor?

Sophia, in a plain dark green frock, showed no sign of avoiding him, and introduced him to her mother, who impressed him; she was delightful and extremely funny. Why did he feel so gloomy?

At twelve they all went out to listen to the sirens and watch the fireworks; Elsa, who was drinking a good deal, clutched him in a rather sentimental pose.

'I hope this will be a better year for us than the last, my darling.'

He was not at all tipsy, and felt little optimism. He would

rather have been kissing Sophia, over there parrying an alcoholic copywriter. She smiled when he got to her.

'Not all that full of joy.'

'You know what Raymond Chandler says – all parties are the same, even the dialogue.'

'You've made a great hit with Mother.'

'I'm bound to say she's made a great hit with me.'

'I'm glad. It was nice of you to be so polite; I thought you would be cold and snubbing after the *Sinterklaas* episode.'

'Haven't you enjoyed yourself?'

'Not a bit. Look at Elsa, fairly basking in adulation. Haven't you seen that the sober ones – you, me, Mother and Herman – have segregated themselves, like Negro schoolchildren?'

'Let's get the hell out of here.'

'Won't it look rude?'

'Nobody will even notice. How did you come?'

'Mother drove me, in my father's car.'

'No, then: we can't go away, but we can put on coats and sit on the deck.'

An hour later Mrs Ter Laan appeared with Herman and joined them.

'Bless my soul, children, aren't you cold?'

'Studying astronomy.'

'Pretty overcast, for astronomy,' said Herman gravely.

Mrs Ter Laan was working her gloves on. 'Lovely to have seen you, my dear, and thank you for a delightful evening. Can we give you a lift, Martin?'

'No thank you very much, Madame, I'll walk – it's not far.'

'You must come out to dinner in Haarlem, and spend the evening.'

'I'll do that, with very great pleasure. Good-night, Herman – happy to have met.'

'Happy days, buster' – grinning. They understood each other and shook hands on it.

Martin had a cup of cocoa, laughing to himself occasionally, and went peacefully to bed. He came half-awake some three

116

hours later, when Elsa arrived, muttering a good deal and taking an unconscionable time to take off her stockings. She was undeniably drunk. It was the first time he could ever remember such a thing. When he got up in the morning she was still asleep after he had called her twice.

He made coffee, and drank two cups himself, sitting thinking, smoking a cigarette peacefully, before going into the bedroom.

'Have some coffee; here, I've brought it in.'

She sat up in sullen disarray and drank, clanking the cup heavily on the saucer in the silence. 'And why didn't you wait for me last night?'

'I could see that you were quite all right, and happily occupied. I did not want to outstay my own welcome, so I went.'

'Are you telling me I stayed too long? – who do you think had to clear the mess up afterwards – I didn't see you helping with that?'

'No, no, I'm sure you didn't stay too long. Quite the contrary.'

'I've told you before that I won't put up with your being vulgar, insulting and gratuitously rude. Rude last night, and insufferably vulgar now.'

'Not at all. I said thank-you-for-a-nice-party like a well-brought-up child.'

'And what about me? It is of no consequence, I suppose, being rude to me.'

She got out of bed and threw off her nightdress in an angry heap.

'I didn't, and don't, think that I had to worry that you wouldn't be looked after.'

'And is that then the behaviour I can expect of the man everyone knows I live with? To go off with that slut, with her winning little ways, and openly leave me to find my own way home?'

'Calling her a slut does not become you. The charming hostess – alcoholic and willing.'

'You humiliated me designedly, because you didn't receive

my undivided attention,' came her voice, muffled by the towel. 'Typically childish.'

'You humiliated yourself. The housekeeper – could you have made it more plain to the eye?'

'Ah. Jealous again. This meaningless, disgusting jealousy that has taken the place of every other feeling towards me.'

Elsa did not appear at her most dignified, standing naked in front of the washbasin, with hanging hair and a pasty face. For the first time, Martin found her ridiculous. He studied her splashing her breasts with cold water, and found it easier than he thought to sound contemptuous. She was tossing clothes about now, hunting for her brassière.

'If you were jealous with a bit of dignity I could bear it, but sometimes you behave towards me as though I were a whore.'

His control snapped. 'After long and careful thought I have concluded that you are a whore.'

Her face contorted with fury; she drew a sobbing breath, thought better of speaking, and after a wild look round grabbed her sewing scissors and came for him.

'Mais ça ne va plus, toi.' He caught the arm reaching at his face, swung her round, and bounced her naked body with a crash on the bed springs. While she was regaining her balance he walked out, put on his hat and coat and went out of the house.

At first he felt joyous and extraordinarily buoyant, and recovered his calm in front of a Vermeer in the Rijksmuseum, a good place for calm. But there were too many people; he went to the rooms of old furniture and tried to think; he sat and smoked a cigarette in the little lobby, staring at the goldfish, and made up his mind; he went out and got a bus to Haarlem.

He did not know the house, and wandered some time around the Frederiksplein; when he found it and rang the bell, an elderly woman disconcerted him by opening and saying abruptly, 'If you want an appointment you should go to the side door.'

118

'I beg your pardon. I wished to see Mademoiselle Ter Laan.'

'Mademoiselle Sophia? I think she is in. Will you come in, and if you don't mind waiting a moment I will go and see.'

A minute later Sophia walked in, wearing trousers and a cardigan with darned sleeves.

'What a nice surprise. Pity Mother's out though; gone to Amsterdam, too.'

'I've left Elsa. And I'm not going back to that house.'

'You don't have to. It's all right, my dear, I understand.'

He found himself crying, a difficult and painful thing for a man, who sobs from the stomach muscles and tears himself to pieces. Sophia pushed him gently on to a sofa, and cuddled him. When he was quiet – 'Come. We are going to spend a pleasant day together. My father is having lunch in the town with some Swedes, so we are alone. I was cooking when you came; I thought I'd make a cake. I'll make coffee now.'

'I'll help you with your cake; I make good cakes.'

'All right,' said Sophia unemotionally, 'and afterwards we'll have a game of chess, extremely lazy, and then we'll go for a walk and talk quietly. Is it a good programme?'

'Yes.'

'Tonight we'll go to the pictures – good picture at the Frans Hals – and you can stay the night, and tomorrow if you want I'll go and get your things.'

In the kitchen he told her what had passed.

'Talk French; old Annie keeps on pottering in and out with fluttering ears, and there's no need to rub it in further how disreputable my friends are.'

'It was the performance last night that finally got it home to me. I sat there for three hours watching her lick her lips. Ironing Herman's shirts, making his bed, making the coffee – "Can I be of any further service, my lord?" Anyone can go and do a housekeeping job, but you don't come back and entertain the guests in the house of an evening, unless you are making it quite plain that you are the mistress there.'

'Yes, of course I've noticed. I've known for weeks and so has Mother. I even wanted to tell you, I was so boiling with rage, but Mother stopped me. She said one must never come between a man and his mistress whatever the circumstances, which is right of course. When I did just that before, you weren't a bit happy; just furious with me.'

'And then coming home drunk – I've never before seen her drunk – and shouting at me for not waiting on her as though I were the footman. Had she really come to think I was such a doormat?'

'Yes. She has said so in this house, a dozen times. You thought she ran away from her husband, to you, and that Erich left out of pride?'

'That's what she always told me.'

'Erich kicked her out, so she came and leeched on to you, and sucked your blood till you had practically none left. She boasted to me that you would never leave her, because you were incapable of living without her. I despaired after I told you – and you wouldn't listen – that she'd declared you to be an incipient alcoholic and an advanced psychotic.

'I thought she'd got you so hogtied – so castrated – that you'd never get away till she'd ruined you completely and just dumped you. Mother didn't believe that would happen – thought you would realize eventually, but that till you did there was nothing I could do. But it was agonizing to watch. You haven't done a stroke of decent work since becoming deeply involved. Jouhandeau knew that, but you wouldn't believe him either. This will be a tremendous blow to her pride, because I'm involved as well – the silly little girl she used to fill with the tales of her cleverness and her conquests.

'As for Herman, Mother talked with him a long while last night, and says he doesn't, in her opinion, care at all sincerely for Elsa. No more single-minded devotion like she got from you. Just something to promote his comforts and amusements, in Mother's view. Who cares? You've broken the spell now.'

'Your move; I've castled.'

'Ho; yes. Where was I? I think the basis of her character — is a thrust — not so much to dominate as to penetrate and absorb. It gives her a thrill for a start to see a roomful of men crawling about after her; she picks one and reduces him to a brainwashed wreck, begging for the privilege of breathing the same air. Look at that poor bastard MacPherson coming back two years after like a dog. If you hadn't been actually living in the house she'd have had him back to play with a bit longer. Look at Marcos, to whom she promised rose-petals and all. She lured him back here, took her clothes off for him once in a hotel room and then gave him *congé*. He'd come here from South America.

'Look at Erich, whom I never knew, but the pattern in the same. She told me with triumph that he used to go on his knees begging her to sleep with him; that if she would he would close his eyes to all that happened. That is the worst. She degrades her men; she despises them. She speaks of them with contempt. I found that unforgivable. They are kindly allowed to make contact with her royal and ancient fanny because she's sexually insatiable, but she does no work for them. Sterilize and paralyse, that's her. Yes, I have grown to hate her. In comparison with her a praying mantis is the Mona Lisa. I don't know whether you've seen my bishop but you're in a spot.'

Sophia won the game.

'I'm out of practice; I'll beat you next time.'

'I'll have let you win,' said Sophia pleasantly. They went for a walk through Haarlem, along the Leidse Vaart and back through the wood.

'Walk on the outside, as though I belonged to you. Good, now I'm your girl.'

'You wanting to give me back some self-respect?'

'That's not a thing I do,' rather tartly. 'You do that for yourself. You've got a lot to learn. First is that when I say things they're true. I don't tell lies.'

'I'm second-hand; doesn't it worry you?'

'I've noticed two things – that you've never been the same with me as with her, and that you've never done the things she told me you would. Her reading of you was all wrong, wrong as the way that she thought about you.'

There was a silence while Martin considered this.

'Where do you want to go?' she asked abruptly.

'Yes. I've been thinking. Perhaps Porquerolles. Middle of winter but that doesn't worry me – won't be any goddam tourists. Probably about two months of uninterrupted mistral, my luck's like that, but I could work.'

'That's what you want – to work and work like stink. How long does it take to write a book?'

'Did one in six weeks once. Saint Jean de Luz. Was I bitten by fleas!'

'Say two months. Say three. Can you live that long? I mean have you money?'

'Yes. What about you? Will you come with me?'

They were in the middle of the wood; nobody was in sight but a depressed old man.

'No, darling, I won't, but give me a kiss. I love you and I'm proud of you.'

When they were back, feeling their hands again after the wet cold, Martin felt courage again in his blood. Sophia was cutting her cake and the tea was on the table when the bell rang.

'Someone smelt the cake.' She went to peep from the window and came back making a face. 'Madam. In person. On warpath. Let me handle her.'

'On the contrary,' said Martin, 'this is my pigeon.' He felt tired, empty of anger, and quite able to handle the situation. His new freedom was about to show itself in an unexpected manner.

For the first time in eight years he saw Elsa come into a room without the familiar, inevitable lift and thrust of his heart. He watched her carefully as she came in, and was quite uninterested. She was very much dressed up – had indeed obviously taken great pains to appear at her best – and was perfectly composed, with a charming smile which she turned on in the darkening room like a lighthouse. Sophia drew the curtains and switched lamps on, with a blank face that denied any feeling at all.

'Hallo,' said Elsa in her pathetic voice; deep, with a catch. 'I thought you'd probably be here.' She kept her hands in her pockets, and her arched, high brows gave her a defenceless look that would ordinarily have been most effective. Her smile was wistful. 'I came to say I was sorry. I was not very pleasant this morning.'

'Would you like some tea?' asked Sophia. 'I've only to fetch an extra cup.'

'Well, if it's no trouble –' When she went out the smile got a bit braver, like a sweet shy rabbit not sure whether it is a success with the children. 'I wasn't feeling bright, but I know I was most disagreeable. I couldn't bear for us to be like that. We've had rows, God knows, but we've always made them up at once.'

'In bed?' She blushed, prettily.

'There or elsewhere.'

'I'm sorry too, for speaking brutally, and I'm glad to see you to tell you.'

Clink went the teacup. 'Thank you,' she said. She cleared her throat. 'I do see what upset you, and I agree that it didn't look good. It was thoughtless of me, and unkind. All the things we share – and have, ever since the war – made it very important to me that I should put it right straight away. To me it is everything; I'm so very – incomplete – without you. It is right in a way too that I should say this in front of Sophia, because I know that she cares for you and that you're very fond of her. I hurt you very much, I know. You see, I feel under a deep obligation to Herman, because he is helping me greatly with this work, which you know has become dreadfully important to me. And in my anxiety I did lose sight of other sides to the question. The three of us are very good friends and I want us to stay that way. And, my darling, we are very deeply belonging to one another; we have weathered so many storms in unison. We are mentally so close, and that is even more important really than the physical closeness, which has always meant so much to us.' She drank her tea in silence.

'Are you staying to supper with Sophia, or shall I expect you? By the way, I haven't of course mentioned anything to Herman that concerns us, but when I was there clearing up this morning he mentioned how struck he'd been at meeting you, and he did suggest just the two of us dropping in tonight for a drink. I didn't know your plans, but I accepted provisionally.' Her voice was normal again, she had negotiated the tricky corners with a choice of words made with care.

'Don't expect me,' said Martin levelly. 'I will not be coming.'

'All right,' cheerfully. 'I'll expect you when I see you.'

'You won't see me again.' She received this with a puzzled look.

'I wish I could say this in a more – less abrupt way, but, you see, I love Sophia.'

'Darling, of course; I know that.'

'No, not that way. I have never slept with her. She's not pregnant either. We must understand each other; I love her. Simply. That means that my life changes. Among other things, it means that I shall not see you again.'

Elsa had got up, and stood now in a characteristic attitude, her shoulders rather hunched, her hands buried deep in her pockets so that they dragged at her coat. She had made an effort to keep her voice natural.

'I feel quite sure that you didn't arrive at this idea alone. My poor darling, you are so vulnerable always. I have wished so often that tiny setbacks in life did not bowl you over so completely. Seeing me talk politely to some strangers – quite disinterestedly, I wasn't at all struck with them – you called me a whore. That is exaggerated talk, but I know you do always express things in an over-emphasized, highly-coloured way. Now you are under rather a strain because we quarrelled, and you are emotionally somewhat attached to Sophia – and I myself am very fond of her – and you talk about love. I'm sure she will agree that that is rather imaginary and unreal, and that she has too much sense to take what you say literally. I know you so well, darling. I haven't had to think deeply over your problems all these years for nothing.'

She glanced towards Sophia, who said and did nothing. Martin had a blue Gauloise in his mouth; that boy smoked too much.

'I'm sorry.' His voice was level. 'I love her; she returns it, we intend to get married as soon as we can, and if I have neuroses and immaturities – likely enough – we are going to handle them together.'

For the first time she began to show irritation in her tone and in the little lines showing round her mouth. Why do men obstinately refuse, suddenly, to listen to the sweet reasonable voice that has sent them for so long peacefully to sleep?

'This is ridiculous; two babes in the wood; deceiving your-selves with these adolescent fantasies.'

'*Pardon; il y a erreur.*' The French made his voice sound amused. 'You might say that I have ceased to deceive myself.'

'Oh, I am not going to play at chopping words, though I know how you enjoy fiddling with them. Too childish and silly. If you could hear yourself talk – a seventeen-year-old student at the debating society. You have grown up so little.' She turned on Sophia, dismissing him as irresponsible. 'I can't help feeling, Sophia, that you have been encouraging Martin in this nonsense, and I must say that I feel it to be disloyal on your part, and not at all what I would have expected of you. Don't you realize that there isn't a single human problem, however tiny, that's come his way in the last five years that I haven't had to solve for him.'

'Possible,' said Sophia gravely, 'and if so quite certainly your fault. From now on he's going to solve his own. You see; he's begun.'

'Oh really! I only wish your mother was here to listen to you. She finds your obstinacy in the face of things you do not understand deplorable.'

'If you have nothing else to say you'd better go,' calmly.

Elsa's face went red, patchily.

'Are you perhaps imagining that I take seriously what a snot-nosed girl says to me, who has done nothing in her short life but sit reading magazines?' She could not prevent herself getting a little shrill towards the end of this long sentence.

'Do not please add to a bad impression by being rude to me in my own house.'

'Your house!'

'Yes, my house, which you will now leave, please. Goodbye.'

'How dare you speak like that to me? Are those your manners? You talk about rudeness?'

Sophia stood up. Her voice sounded unusually deep. 'I dare speak like that, and more, to whores. Out!'

Elsa stood a moment rooted, then turned abruptly and walked out. The furious tap of her heels sounded like pistol shots in the high tiled hall; the street door snapped to like teeth. Silence.

'Ow!' Martin was shaking his fingers up and down loosely, in the classic French gesture. Sophia looked at the little lines of irony in his face. Not so childish, she thought.

'Yes, she lost control.' She stood with her arms crossed on her breast, frowning. 'To be just, so did I. But it was overdone and made me sick. The deliberate effort to keep you immature and at an emotional level. But she had no reason to suppose that you wouldn't fall for the melting eye, the weeping voice, the beautiful garden of flowerlike thoughts. She has lost sight of you. And we intend to get married – at the earliest opportunity wasn't it? I'm not so convinced, my boy. Still –' She frowned again, and then burst out laughing. 'Babes in the wood! I wasn't going to forgive the old cow that.'

Martin's ironic face was directed towards her now. 'You

aren't going to marry me just to spite her, are you? How did I do?'

'You didn't do badly. A bit pompous; that debating society remark was a naughty one. But you weren't rude, as I was. You were nervous, and that stiffened you up. It was an effort, wasn't it? Never mind, console yourself. Your *adieu* to the Matthew Marisstraat.'

A little under three months later Sophia stepped off the boat from Hyères on to the island of Porquerolles. The mistral was blowing hard. The sun shone on a roughened sea and the boat pitched sharply, but she looked unruffled. She kissed him warmly.

'You do smell offensively of garlic,' she said, 'and I really think you might have shaved.'

Part Three

The House of Keeping

Martin slept very soundly; when he woke he could remember
having had ridiculous dreams, but not the details. The night
before, and the unreal quality of everything, had penetrated
his sleep. The flat in the Josef Israelskade, and the furniture
piled as though for a remover's lorry; Van der Valk's face
lined and sepulchral in the dim old reflections of Elsa's dressing table; the policeman's talkative, ironic voice talking with
horrid familiarity to a corpse. And his hand holding the two
packets of photos; Elsa's secret behind the looking-glass. There
had been, too, another envelope of photos, of him, in the
writing-desk that lay now in pieces. Were these also him? The
policeman had spoken to Elsa, and had said 'Our friend'. Who
was our friend? Was it him? On the border between sleep and
life Martin had no idea.

He dressed and shaved as usual, and had breakfast – two
slices with cheese and one with gingerbread – waiting rather
stupidly for a revelation. No angel appeared, but at nine
o'clock sharp Van der Valk did, and called him into the office.
It was one of the official mornings, a neat folder of typed
sheets lay on the desk.

'You must listen carefully,' the policeman intoned, 'and stop
me if there is anything you query or challenge.' He read in a
flat monotone; *procès verbal*. It all sounded quite meaningless.
A chief inspector of police with a bored intelligent face and an
expensive suit leaned against the window frame and watched
for a while; looks like a man who takes bribes, thought
Martin resentfully. He felt more resentful still when there was
a muttered conference at the end of the room, both of them

staring at him.

Van der Valk looked fresh and rested, but stayed mono-syllabic. Finally he told Martin to wait in the guard's office, gathered up his papers and went into the chief inspector's room. Martin hung about waspishly for nearly an hour, but was relieved when Van der Valk reappeared finally, smiling and gay.

'We're off to see the wizard,' he said, 'hold on to your hats.' Martin followed him back to the *recherche* office.

'Right. Two things. I can tell you something now. There was another lover, not you. He exists, is probably here in this town, and we hope to make his acquaintance suddenly. Maybe within a couple of days. Now this has to be done sharpish. He may realise – don't say will – that we've rumbled something in the Josef Israels, and try a bunk. I don't know his name, what he looks like, or anything about him, except his hobby. Might be his business.'

'Which is? Tell, you're killing me.'

'Photography,' said Van der Valk with a ferocious grin. Lion, seeing Christian that got away. 'Now I've told the chief inspector what I know, and think; he agrees, Catchee catchee. Now follow closely; this may seem rough on you, but I think and you'll see that it's not as silly as it sounds. If this chap has any idea we're on to him he breaks, and we're in the shit. We might not get him; lot of agonized telephoning to frontiers, passport people in a stew, and the fellow walks through be-cause nobody's quite sure what he's looking for. So to provide a smokescreen I'm charging you officially with this crime. Now take it easy. I said I know this man exists. To pin an identity on him and produce him is another matter. Till then you're it. We hand out to the Press that you are charged in face of a strong case against you, and that the examining magistrate is questioning you – this has all the advantage of being perfectly true – and that he will doubtless release such details of the horrid crime as he thinks fit, all in good time. All laid on thick and lavish. Object: to keep our man sleeping peacefully on his two ears till I am shaking hands with him. I say all this to reassure you; we're not leaving you for ever in the cold night air. Further, you'll see your wife shortly at the Palais de Justice and you can explain the situation. After that you'll be *au secret* and will see nobody. You'll doubtless be remanded to the Huis van Bewaring and may even be exercised alone. You'll be allowed no visitors and your letters will be censored. Not to worry; it won't be that long. Just stay quiet and be patient.

'Point number two. The examining magistrate doesn't know about this piece of evidence I have. You might be tempted to tell him. Don't. You would step off for the killing of de Charmoy. I'll make this clear. He is insisting on your being charged, in direct contradiction to my report that you are not, once we pass superficial appearances, guilty of any damn thing at all. The examining magistrate, in fact, has a theory that the police are a lot of tea-drinking hacks who are quite likely to arrest the wrong geyser. That I in particular think myself too smart and foul up a simple affair with fancy theories. He talks about "police psychological insight" in a special tone of voice.

'Now we are just a tiny bit jealous of our good name. Very well, he insists on having you – he's getting you; we turn you over to him. We intend to put our photographic pal in the bag and then jump out shouting, *"Paas Haas"* and make him eat his *toupet*. So what you have to remember in this. He – the magistrate – has the record of everything, pretty well, that's been said or done – except last night. I've had you in the Josef Israels all right for one reason or another – but for your neck, *jongen,* you saw no search and you know nothing about photos. I haven't shown you them and I'm not going to. Just remember, *jongen,* don't sell us out, and we won't sell you out. Right, we are now going to provide picturesque details.'

Van der Valk snapped a handcuff on his wrist. Cuffed ostentatiously together they went out to the little Volkswagen.

Several cameras clicked with enthusiasm. At the Palais de Justice they made, Martin thought, quite an impressive entrance.

He was brought into a kind of lobby filled with the uniforms of the state police, with their blue breeches and facings. In an inner office he was signed for – received in good condition one body – and left to cool his heels while Van der Valk made small-talk. The state police eyed him stonily. He was ready to become impatient when Van der Valk came back and steered him across a hallway full of lawyers in tatty robes, most with bands that could have done with a wash. There was one young and pretty woman, her bands shining white; that's the one for me, he thought. His confidence had been a bit daunted by the surroundings, but revived when they came to a waiting-room with benches, and he saw Sophia, formal in a black suit. She gave him a wide anxious smile.

Van der Valk sat casually within earshot and brought out a crumpled morning paper.

'Got to be someone with you while you talk; pay no attention; better me than one of these lunks.'

Sophia gave a questioning look.

'It's a plot of some kind. Everything's all right and they are sure it isn't me, and it won't ever come to trial; this is a smokescreen, but I can't help feeling a bit dubious.'

'Boo, I'm not surprised you feel dubious. I feel like what's his name, in Dickens, at the riverside where they find the bird of prey.'

'Eugene. Two forgeries, three burglaries and a midnight assassination. I feel guilty as hell but I'll explain. Look, he's found something in the Josef Israels. I'm not allowed to know what it is, but it confirms his idea. There is a someone to whom this death points very strongly, once anybody knows he exists. Elsa kept it a secret. He isn't identified yet. Now it's very important this fellow should not be alarmed, so for security and police politics, and to satisfy the prosecutor, who doesn't know he exists, I have to be charged. It goes to the

Press and the villain sleeps sound, until, we hope, the posse arrives at full gallop. I don't feel too happy, but Van der Valk says he's quite confident.'

Sophia kissed him. 'I suppose I do understand, though it seems peculiar, and you'll be crucified in the Press. That's only just, I suppose. We read about other people's mishaps with greedy eyes: we squirm when we are put up on the bandstand. Will it be very awful for you?'

'Don't think so; better than police stations, maybe. I have to sit in the Huis van Bewaring – sinister name, huh, the House of Keeping? Nice fresh air on the Weteringschans. I can't see you and my letters will be censored, but he says only two weeks. Can you give me some money and tobacco?'

'I brought both. Shag best, hey? How much money – a couple of *tientjes*?'

'Plenty. You look good.'

'Yes, I thought a white collar would show the blood better.'

It was like waiting for a train, thought Martin. Why was it that on these occasions one could speak nothing but banalities?

However she had understood, and if he could trust Van der Valk to keep him from being tried and possibly condemned, he could trust him, presumably, to save Sophia from unnecessary anxiety. He turned to him.

'Let's get it over then,' rather impatiently; like a good policeman he was deep in football.

'That bloody useless Ajax lost again.'

Martin gave Sophia his best kiss. 'Remember Cyrano: *"Les vers du vieux Baro valant moins que zéro – Je les interromps sans remords."* ' As he was marched along by a state policeman he thought of another quotation, Marshal Ney's remark on getting into a tight spot at the battle of Jena: 'The wine is poured, and we must drink it.' Down they went to the basement.

There was a row of mean little cells, lit only by tiny tunnels barely above ground level; through the thick little pane he could guess at opaque daylight.

'Want to go to the lavatory?' asked the policeman indifferently. They were not like the ordinary police, these ones, with their slightly theatrical uniforms. Their boots were too highly polished, and had more of a look of the office than of the street; their faces were pale and shadowed, their hands white and uncalloused. Altogether they had the greasy, papery, unventilated texture of law-courts; they even smelt of paper, and, slightly, of disinfectant. Martin decided with emphasis that he preferred police bureaux. He missed the boisterous earthy jokes, the uninhibited yawning and scratching, and the vulgar slurping of hot coffee; sympathetic farmyard sounds of digestion and well-being. 'Damn this crowd; look as if they put paper instead of cheese on their bread at breakfast-time.'

He was kept about twenty minutes before the familiar clank of keys brought him out of a completely absorbed reverie. *Camino real,* he thought, obeying the grunts behind him. 'Right . . . up the stairs . . . left . . . stop.' They were in a wide corridor on the first floor, above the courtrooms and the lawyers, standing on highly polished parquet, and facing highly polished panelling. There was a little alcove with a wooden bench, polished by many apprehensive pairs of trousers; the butler signed to him to sit. He found himself gazing at a door with a discreet official plate: 'Mr. J. F. R. Slotemaker de Bruin. Officier van Justitie.' Face to face with the bogyman at last.

The Officer of Justice in Holland is a functionary whose duties correspond exactly neither to those of the Procureur de la République nor of the Juge d'Instruction. He combines largely the duties of both, that is to say he sifts evidence with a view to compiling an eventual prosecution, and in the court itself he prosecutes. But he does not accompany police inquiries in a criminal case on the scene, nor does he hand over his dossier at, so to speak, the courtroom door. In a sense he is like the District Attorney in America, but his is a purely judicial and in no sense political post; he is appointed and not elected. One does not suddenly find Dutch magistrates popping up playing to the crowd, and while they interview and are interviewed by the Press they are given neither to god-like pronouncement nor folksy comment. In a large city such as Amsterdam there will be several of these personages. Like all members of a judiciary they vary greatly in outlook from the liberal and progressive to the rigid reactionary.

The butler slipped out of the door and holding it barely ajar behind him beckoned to Martin. It was like a defaulters' parade in the army – he quite expected. ''Ats off', but inside the resemblance vanished abruptly.

The large comfortable office was panelled like the passage and filled with books. No sign of filing cabinets, nor of any bureaucratic nonsense, except that on the big, beautifully gleaming, walnut writing table lay a green cardboard folder. The man behind the table sat at an angle, and the table itself was at an angle to the window. A vase of freesias stood on the table, and in the window embrasure was another with four long-stemmed roses. It was a delightful room, high and sunny and civilized, a room for study, for conversation and for music.

The man behind the desk was reading a typed document as the butler ushered Martin in, and did not look up. Martin, standing in front of the table, had a moment to examine this new, formidable adversary. He had never been so surprised in his life.

From Van der Valk's words he had pictured an old man, whom he had imagined as something like Neville Chamberlain to look at, intelligent but old-fashioned, rigid, righteous in a narrow-minded way, obstinate, and a bully. Dressed doubtless in a black coat and probably – even now – a wing collar. This was an old gentleman, certainly, if the description fitted an upright, thin man of sixty. A narrow, but calm even serene face, every line showing character and intelligence. Reminded him of Conrad, both of them, Veidt and Adenauer too. His hands were long, fine and brown, one holding a very good cigar indeed, he noticed enviously. He wore a palish grey suit and a white silk shirt; his tie was patterned with rose and grey diamonds. He wore a plain gold wristwatch and a broad wedding ring; on his left hand a worn signet set with small diamonds.

When he raised his eyes they were a clear greenish grey, and the skin was not parchment but young and tanned, the skin of a man who spends much time on boats. His hair was the colour of his cigar-ash, cut short. He wore horn-rims, and smoked without a holder, and without sucking his cigar-end.

He spoke, in a quiet but not soft voice, very good Dutch with a tendency to use French words. 'Yes. Well –' He put down the sheets, still studying Martin with even eyes.

'Forgive me. I had to read it, but I did not wish to keep you waiting outside my door.' He stood up and gave a slight, grave bow, astonishing Martin.

'Molenaar, perhaps you could do us the kindness of fetching a chair.'

Martin sat, with a feeling of having been shot through the heart. The magistrate pulled open a drawer, and put an unopened packet of Everests on the guest's side of the table.

'Please smoke if you feel inclined. I fear I have had my coffee, otherwise I should certainly offer you some, since the young woman who brings it is most obliging.' Martin did not take a cigarette, though he wanted one badly. 'This is too good. This is *la chansonette* carried to the level of art.'

'Now, if it is agreeable to you we will have a conversation. I hope it does not embarrass you to have the state police officer present, but I can assure you that he is absolutely discreet. It is a rule that we must respect.' He gave a smile, pleasantly ironic. 'I must receive occasionally in this office persons ill disposed towards me. They tend to believe that I will punish them, an embodiment of a vengeful society. They would like to feel vengeful too – get it in first, perhaps. Justice has of course a punitive as well as a protective aspect; it is unavoidable. Above the door of the Old Bailey, which is the rather fanciful name – but of course you are aware – given to the central criminal court of London, is written: "Protect the children of the poor and punish the wicked." Very often the two coincide.'

He drew on his cigar. 'I should on the whole prefer it if my duties precluded the second clause. Mm. You are thinking me tedious, and pompous. However, this is your introduction to the administration of justice in the Kingdom of the Netherlands. It requires, I believe, an explanation. Your individual views and my own must be submitted to the scrutiny and decision of the state. Too many people, alas, are not informed of the care with which the state considers affairs. In this instance the Press is not free from blame. The functionaries of the state, myself for instance, are not blameless either. People see too often the *longueurs*, the delays, the stupidities.' He made again a tiny bow towards Martin. 'We shall, I hope, find ourselves able to eliminate most of these.'

Martin felt uplifted by the magistrate's manners and the eighteenth-century feeling of reason. He felt himself in the presence of Talleyrand.

'Sir, I am very appreciative of your courtesy.' The magistrate broke the seal on the packet of Everests, drew a cigarette out halfway, and presented it gravely. Martin took it, feeling himself surrender. 'I am afraid that you have formed an impression of my guilt. That is very serious for me, since it is a murder.'

The magistrate looked at his freesias. 'You must not allow yourself to think that. I have no opinion about your guilt; such a presupposition would be immoral. I have, you may allow me to say, an impression that you acted imprudently; that is sufficiently demonstrated, I think, by the circumstances in which you find yourself at the Palais de Justice. Your motives may be perfectly pure, you have possibly done things you regret, and which of us has not. Some hasty actions have deplorable consequences. But your speaking like that warns me that you have come here with a false notion, possibly, of me. Have you perhaps been told that I was autocratic and overbearing?' Eyebrow and mouth went up together at the corner. 'Conceivably by Inspector Van der Valk?'

Martin felt harassed. Nobody's idiot, this man. He thought of the loyalty he promised the policeman. He had been warned, but damn it, he had expected a different reception, chilly and hostile. This was more complicated.

'I don't think the inspector threatened me at all. But an Officer of Justice – the idea is alarming.'

The magistrate smiled, his ironic smile. 'I think I had better define my position. I will be didactic, I trust not pedantic. Pedantry is an error in law. It flaws the English system, admirable as it is in many ways. I am bound, yes, to view an event such as a murder with severe eyes. I must take pains to ensure that whoever does such things is brought, and speedily, to account for his actions as he best may. In this position you find yourself at present. I have felt uneasy for some days that you were held at the disposal of the police; it is irregular. I thought your position unclear and illogical; you ought to have had it made clearer to you how you stood. Inspector Van der Valk was unwilling that you should be charged when he was by no means satisfied that you were in fact responsible for any legal misdeed. I agreed and agree; I was willing to allow him latitude in what he felt to be a moral issue. The legal aspect does not coincide exactly with the moral aspect. Legally, since nobody has appeared to answer for this crime, you must now be placed in an unambiguous situation, designed to protect your interests quite as much as those of the state.

'I have another function, definable as the examination of a man once apprehended, endeavouring to make clear the sequence of events bearing upon his possible answerability. If it appears that events determine his authority for what the state terms a crime, it is my further duty to pursue him before a tribunal as the state allows.

'I do not' – again the ironic smile – 'gather scalps, nor feel that I win or lose, and count the days thereby good or bad.

138

You will have noticed that this is the attitude of the police. There is nothing unethical in that; their duty is to lay hands on those they believe to be wrong-doers. These beliefs, built on a chain of probabilities, are hasty and superficial; this cannot be otherwise, for they live under pressure of time and crowds. Yielding, understandably, to these pressures, policemen and other officers use methods that can be thought disreputable. This fact brings me into occasional conflict with the police; they may feel sometimes that I am hostile to them.

'You are right to be guarded in replying to my query about Inspector Van der Valk; he is a man of considerable gifts, whom I admire for his integrity. But I feel that in his efforts to grasp all the details of an obscure happening he has left you too long with no more than a vague certainty that you are connected with this woman. I had to insist that this should stop. I am not pursuing you; I wish that to be clear.'

'There is then no presumption of my guilt?'

'None whatever.'

'Then I can, surely, be released, Sir?'

'There is, unfortunately, no presumption of your innocence,' said the magistrate without sarcasm. 'There is doubt, and an open mind. You recall my saying that our individual views must be submitted to the decision of the state. The state provides that a person coming under imputation of a hand in violent death must be held at the state's disposal until obscurities can be examined. The charge that brings you to my office is a formal document setting out the state's intention and the reasons supporting this. A subpoena, scarcely more. It means neither that you are guilty nor that I think you so. Simply that I am not satisfied, that I do not understand your role in the affair. I hope you find me lucid.'

'Yes. Yes, I understand. May I say that I have confidence in you?'

'That is a generous remark, which helps me greatly. You may be inclined, during the coming days, to feel discouraged, but you may be reassured that we shall understand.'

The magistrate lit another cigar with attention. 'We have overcome a great difficulty. If you felt that you were treated in a harsh and rigid manner, you would be disinclined to reply freely to my questions. These are bound to be searching and painfully personal. No man wants his life scrutinised by an examination which if intelligently conducted is cruel and if stupidly is brutal. A doctor is obliged to ask such questions, but the situation is different; his patient has sought him out of his own free will, feels himself oppressed, and hopes for relief from anxiety and pain alike. Officials of the Government such as myself are gardeners – the thought is the German Chancellor's, I believe he has a fine garden at Rhondorf. We must weed, prune, disturb sensitive roots. A transplanted flower hangs its head, lets fall leaves, may die before it can flower again. Healing can be a painful process.'

For a moment he collected his thoughts, looking out of the window. Then he sighed and opened the file on his table.

'Paper, paper; heartless stuff. I myself greatly dislike putting my signature to anything; I feel that I have surrendered an integral fraction of myself. Good. The puzzling and troublesome feature of this affair has been the non-appearance of any other person who is really involved at all. Usually' – the smile again – 'we are pestered by an embarrassing number of persons who have acted in a silly or suspicious manner. We face a woman who could be presumed to have a large acquaintance, and nobody has seen her to any purpose in a considerable time.'

This was all stale cake to Martin. He had been delighted and impressed by the little homily on the ethics of jurisprudence, but on this ground he feared that the magistrate would lack Van der Valk's homely and earthy style of illustration. He listened with attention, but without the ability to take it very seriously. It had happened to someone else. Detachment first, then boredom.

The magistrate's voice, lucid, brief, detailed characters, movements, actions and reactions; it had all, suddenly, sprung from the pages of a dull book. Bouwman, Herman, Erich van Kampen; all were peeled neatly away from their attachment to an 'incident'. Martin realized with clarity that according to the depositions, which were incontestable, nobody, literally nobody, had been on the scene. As the voice summarized the movements and enquiries of Van der Valk in the days following Elsa's death he saw himself increasingly isolated. Depression seized him. The scrutiny of the state — and this delightful gentleman with his logical mind was preparing to tell him: 'It does not look as though you killed her, but we are compelled to believe that you did.' A bad melodrama.

'They were just ready to throw Bulldog Drummond into the pool with the crocodiles, but the villain went on too long with his flowery speech (embodying a full confession) and Algy or Biggles or whoever it was would shout "Hold on, Old Son".' He was in that position. When Algy did come it would be carrying a camera, according to Van der Valk. 'Someone, anyone, appear and get me out of this! Raymond Chandler wrote somewhere, cheerfully, 'When in doubt have a man come in the door with a gun in his hand.' Don't let me down, Raymond!'

Daydreaming, he missed whole sentences as the magistrate spoke; once he contradicted himself very stupidly indeed. He felt hot and flustered. The magistrate looked at him, neither with sympathy nor without. Professional, anti-sym and anti-anti. Here, we are professionally impathetic.

'You are tired and you are not doing yourself justice. We had better in any case call a halt; there are numerous other persons waiting for me to decide what, to some degree, will shape their next few days.'

He closed the file and pulled on his cigar. 'Looks sticky, doesn't it?'

The colloquialism was unexpected. Martin had realized that he was being brainwashed. This was a professional inquisitor, expert in disarmament.

'I have come to a conclusion, which is that I cannot justify

141

setting you free. I must therefore write an advice to the Director of the House of Keeping, where I am sure that in the long term you will be best placed. You will be quiet; quiet is what we all need. I shall ask you to come and see me daily at a fixed hour each morning. In an orderly and patient manner we will unravel together some points that are still obscure to me. I can be quite sure that you will benefit from these coming days. At present you are very tired.'

Martin stood up and bowed; the magistrate returned the gesture, and walked over to his window, where he examined his freesias.

'Do not worry. You may feel convinced that the truth will appear, and the truth, you feel certain, will establish the innocence which you maintain. Patience is needed. Molenaar, you might see to my friend, will you?'

As Martin was ushered out by the butler, whose presence he had entirely forgotten, he saw the magistrate pensively lighting another cigar.

He had twenty minutes again in the mousehole down in the basement, before the door was opened again. This time it was out the back way, into a yard. A minibus stood waiting, driver and guard in state police uniforms. Presumably the less intelligent among them did all this footman stuff; it had not occurred to him before. He shrugged; somebody had to empty the dustbins too; at the moment he was, figuratively, a dustbin. Two or three depressed characters sat in the bus.

The guard collected a large manila envelope and locked the doors; the driver smoked, surreptitiously; on the way to the Weteringschans, nobody spoke; they swayed together in a half-felt comradeship, vibrating in unison to the quiet simmer of the motor at red lights, lurching in unison at green. The driver had his cigarette between the fingers of his left hand; it made his gearshifting pretty sloppy.

There was no fuss; the guard got down yawning and rang the bell, and the now-familiar jingle of keys and bolts came faintly through. At the time Martin was struck by the sense of *déjà-vu* as he passed through an ante-room and up a flight of stone steps to a corridor outside an office. It was some hours later that it struck him with amusement how like a convent it all was.

The three or four of them sat like schoolchildren on a wooden form, outside an ordinary ground-glass door. The policeman delivered his envelope and strode off hitching at his breeches in a bucolic way; he could be heard laughing and chatting in a room down the passage. Talk broke out; cigarettes were lit and police stations compared in a worldly-wise way.

It seemed that they had all suffered torments in dark and filthy holes with uneatable food, browbeaten and generally treated with brutality. Martin stayed quiet after distributing his last tailormades; he recognized the normal bragging of scared children, but disliked the chattiness, and when a petty embezzler asked with undue familiarity, 'What they got you for, tosher?' he answered, 'Murder, tosher,' and there was an awestruck silence before they went back to agreeing that all examining magistrates were sarcastic, sadistic, and bastards to a man.

After a few minutes a sort of clerk, in ordinary clothes, popped his head out and called a name. Each took ten or fifteen minutes; he was the third. Nobody watched them; it was friendly and casual.

It was an ordinary business office inside, very Dutch; white paint, plenty of fresh air, grey metal furniture, window-boxes and flowerpots. A desk for the clerk, busy at a noiseless typewriter, and a desk for a sort of commissaire, a big, sturdy-shouldered Dutch business man in the grey suit and tie with speckles that is the uniform of Dutch business men (outside, a soft grey hat). There was nothing penal in the atmosphere.

The commissaire nodded pleasantly and told him to sit down. His tone was calm, brisk and reassuring.

'The Officer of Justice has asked me to commit you to the House of Keeping while your affair is under his consideration. Do you realize what this means?'

'Broadly. I'm not up on the details.'

'Ahah. It's the usual and normal method of handling these judicial preliminaries. Houses such as these hold a large number of people who are in a situation like yours, either awaiting trial or not yet committed. It is not a prison or a house of reform. You are locked up and that is all. Just what the name implies. There are some persons who have committed minor offences and whom it is not thought necessary to send to a prison, or not worth the trouble. You can have a cell to yourself or be with two or three others; any preference?'

'By myself, if you don't mind.'

'I agree; advisable anyhow. The magistrate hasn't made any order that you should be kept *au secret*; I see no necessity, but it's better to be alone. Now it is clearly advisable that you should be here; these affairs are often lengthy. There is no hardship; the rules are explicit and must be kept, but that is no hardship. You wear your own clothes; for ease in administration you get underclothes and towels from us. Now, formally, have you any objection to this course of action?'

'Can't think of any,' grinned Martin.

The man grinned back. 'That's the trick. Now tell me, what about a lawyer? I've got a list here, you can pick whom you like, he has full access to you and you can see him in private, naturally. The point hasn't been brought up earlier since you were only charged this morning. Any ideas?'

'Don't really want a lawyer; not yet anyhow. Haven't bothered hitherto and can't really think it necessary now. You see, I deny this all obstinately – I hope that the magistrate will come to agree with me!'

The commissaire pulled a face, then laughed. 'I admire your faith in Dutch justice, but, you know, even so I'd advise you to have someone, a professional who understands legal technicalities. The magistrate might refuse to question you on certain subjects unless your lawyer were present. There are complex rules governing procedures in criminal cases, and a lawyer would advise you how you might avoid prejudicing yourself. However, you needn't make your mind up instantly, but give it careful thought.'

It jogged on. Martin gave a few possessions into the care of another official, and was rather indignant when he was not allowed to keep his pen; when he found a ballpoint in a side pocket that nobody had noticed he felt able to laugh at bureaucracy. He was searched in a casual, unconvinced manner and finally introduced through a second heavy door into the 'House' itself.

Here he received underclothes, eating implements – several odd objects; very like the army. He was taken by a warder to his room, on the second of several floors built round a large central hallway. Except for locks and bolts, it could have been a hostel for the unemployed poor, run by thrifty and benevolent nuns. He got an hour to acclimatize himself undisturbed before a sort of Reverend Mother in blue overalls and rimless glasses walked in and asked whether everything was all right with him. Tea and sympathy.

At intervals afterwards other nuns appeared, carrying library books, little printed pamphlets of instructions and information, food – bread with a generous piece of sausage and two lots of coffee. Prisoners served the food – not prisoners, kept persons. After food, washing water and a question whether he would like some cell work.

'You can earn some money; only wrapping soap, and it passes the time. Concentrates your mind.' Like being hanged, thought Martin, remembering the opinion of Doctor Johnson.

For an hour or two in the evening the loudspeaker relayed music from a radio somewhere, and one could make one's bed up and lie on it if one felt so inclined. Martin read comfortably till ten and warning bells; bedtime, *jongens*. He slept better than he had for a month, since before the Tuesday night when Elsa had been killed and he had gone home shrugging, thinking perhaps it was better anyway not to see her in person. What had happened in that room above the street? Whose eyes had noticed him standing below? Why had death been the result? Could a murder have been a consequence – how he could not see – of his having stood there? Had he been the unwitting – admitted – indirect – admitted – but nevertheless actual cause of Elsa's death? What would the consequence be for him, if that were so?

'I invite your close attention,' the voice was saying; Mr J. F. R. Slotemaker de Bruin. 'We are going to examine various details with care. In your conversations with Inspector Van der Valk you talk, frequently, about imagination. You invited him to use his own, and you used yours, to considerable purpose. This appeal you wish to extend to me, no doubt. I may say that I dislike the imagination. I wish you to make a conscious effort, avoid your imagination scrupulously, and use your processes of thought.'

'Not much difference that I can see.'

'My dear friend, everybody has an intellect of sorts. Everybody has an imagination, the power to project an image upon the mind. Your power is unusually active and vivid. That can be a misfortune.'

'Are you telling me I imagine things, and then present them as the truth?' Martin's voice was indignant.

'It would not be unusual. But do not put words into my mouth; you imagine that I suggest the notion; it is an example of what I am telling you. Your imagination is confused hopelessly with your intellect. You used a word in one of your statements: unthinkable.'

'Probably.'

'What you meant was unimaginable. There is a world of difference. Your statements ask me – it is implied continually – to imagine a situation. If the situation so imagined is sufficiently vivid and striking, you mean to go on, I can accept it as the truth. You appear to forget that I must apply a more stringent test before I can accept these stories. They must satisfy not only my imagination but my intellect.

'This woman, whom I never saw nor knew. I can't imagine her, her actions and reactions, very readily, but only through the medium of your mind. I wish to inquire into her more closely – can I in fact *think* these things? Can my intellect accept them, in the light of facts about her that I possess – or are they unthinkable?'

'I am not following you very closely.'

'Exactly. You are not in the habit of thinking. You reverse what should be a normal process. If your imagination accepts a proposition, you see no reason to ask your brain to examine it as well. The intellect is lazy. Imagination steps into its place; a good stick but a bad crutch, as the English say.'

'I still haven't grasped properly what you want of me.'

'Are you acquainted with a cartoonist called Herge?'

'Yes, of course.'

'He creates,' went on the magistrate, imperturbable, 'a boy called Tintin. An imbecile-looking and undernourished adolescent. This boy is superbly observant; indeed he draws brilliant conclusions from the scantiest of premises. He is expert with every imaginable mechanical contrivance. He survives appalling hardships and disasters uninjured and unfatigued. He tackles organized bodies of armed and desperate criminals, and disrupts them completely. With his friends, a drunken sailor and an absent-minded professor – classic figures, pure genius – he is plunged into appalling jeopardy. Not only gangsters but material objects are banded against them, and leap out at them. When all else is conquered they are placed in fresh and terrifying hazard by two singularly cretinous – I speak from wide experience – policemen.

'There is nothing,' he said with relish, 'I enjoy more than reading these enchanting books to my grandchildren. You know them?'

'Certainly,' said Martin, tickled into laughter.

'Brilliantly imagined, and most dexterously realized in pen and colour. But – is it not so? – quite unthinkable.'

'I see.'

'Well, my friend, you invite my consideration in your statements of things worthy of Captain Haddock.'

'Nevertheless, I have told the truth.' Martin's voice had a stubborn honesty.

'Truth. It can be true, however much it seems untrue. I do not reject your words. Your constructions hang together, are ingenious and entertaining – much like the inventions of the admirable Professor Tournesol. I wish to know if they are real. Your recollections of your life with this woman, even of the events leading up to the night on which she died, are true in your eyes. Now will you consider, with your intellect, the possibility that your imagination has coloured these events and insisted that this account is the truth?'

There was a silence.

'It is the truth as I saw it,' said Martin slowly. 'I cannot go further than that.'

'You and I,' said the magistrate amicably, 'are going to get along. Truth does not exist, in the accounts of witnesses of an exciting event. Even the most innocent, the hardest headed, the best balanced. Their sense of time is distorted; they will swear that a sequence that cannot logically have taken less than five minutes was all over in thirty seconds. They will swear that a room was empty, when three persons have entered and left again. Asked to say rather that they did not notice, they become indignant, as you did, thinking I am impugning not only their honesty but their sound, reliable senses. In a really dreadful disaster, such as the Mercedes crash at Le Mans in fifty-five, nobody's word can be relied upon as to what really happened. Except the dead man's. The witness, the one witness who is not available at the judicial inquiry. That particular man was, by the way, a hero on that occasion.'

A motor-racing fan, thought Martin; complex character. 'I have thought, or perhaps imagined, all sorts of things about this,' he said. 'I have even wondered whether I had in reality killed the woman and suppressed the memory entirely. Blackout killings have been known.'

'Sounds rather like Captain Haddock,' commented the magistrate, lighting a cigar. Martin grinned, admitting that one.

'I can arrange an investigation into your state of mind. What jargon terms a psychiatric search. These are, as you are aware, used very freely nowadays, often to establish a person's suitability for an exacting position. One might say that a murderer is in an exacting position, hm? We might find out interesting things, such as your possible aptitude for this crime. Most of all some bearing on your statements as evidence. What sort of witness you make. Apart from what you yourself have told us – this is why the reliability of your words is crucial – any evidence against you is circumstantial, which means of little use. Quite apart from ethics' – the ironic smile – 'it is difficult to present such a case to the judges.

'However, it is certainly my duty to tell you that such a search, angled towards your contacts with this woman, could compromise you very deeply. You would be severely cross-examined. I have the right to do the same thing, certainly, but I do not judge the occasion suitable.'

Martin breathed deeply with his eyes shut, like a boxer between rounds. 'Would this examination be voluntary, or would you order it?'

'I could order it; I frequently do. But your voluntary acceptance of the idea is valuable. A lawyer might say that I was trying to trick you into it. Would you wish first to take advice?'

'What would he say, the lawyer?'

'He would very likely protest at the way I am speaking to you, saying that I was holding out inducements and promises. A refinement of the *chansonette*. I merely state the point.'

'If the findings were hostile to me could I get another independent inquiry?'

'You could,' placidly.

'I don't want a lawyer,' said Martin abruptly.

'Indeed,' said the magistrate calmly, 'I cannot see that you need one.'

'In all honesty,' said Martin, 'I have told no lies. But could an inquiry of this kind really show inaccuracy in my stories?'

'It would fill in lacunae, possibly pointing to inaccuracy. You realize that I could, simply by questioning you, do the same thing, very likely. But that would only encourage you to use your imagination further; not at all what I want. To trip you up, to confuse you into contradicting yourself, would be easy, and also quite futile.'

'Let's do it,' said Martin. 'Everything on the red.'

'When you gamble you should only do so on what is as near a certainty as you can contrive. Is that the case?'

'Yes, I think it is.'

'Since you persist in a figurative comparison, remember that I am the casino. I take a percentage of all sums gambled. Very well. I shall have transcripts made of all the relevant documents, which I shall send to the clinic for the chief's consideration. If he agrees that a search would be of value – since he is a busy man – I shall arrange for it to take place as soon as may be. There will, I think, be little point in my seeing you again till the findings become available to me.'

There was a small pause; Martin stubbed out his cigarette.

'Will you answer a question of mine, Sir?'

'I will.'

'If these findings go against me, will you institute proceedings?'

'In the absence of any further evidence, and if by "against you" you mean that compromising inconsistencies are shown to exist in your statement, I think it likely that I shall.'

'And if there are no discrepancies?'

'That, my friend, had better wait till the findings are made. I hold out no inducement and I will make no promise. But under certain circumstances I might consider releasing you provisionally.'

'Forgive me, but may I know those provisions?'

'Certainly. You would be required to hold yourself at my disposal, and at that of the police, till the case was officially closed. You would be asked to surrender your passport, and

150

establish your presence in your home by a daily report to the local bureau. You would have to bear in mind that I may, should I think fit, bring you again into the cutody of the House of Keeping. This sounds discouraging, I know, and I must emphasize that the discovery of fresh evidence could at any time change the face of affairs completely.'

'But in the absence of evidence, you would, eventually, release me?'

The magistrate leaned his face on his hand and studied him. 'Have you thought that a situation might in certain circumstances arise in which a moral certainty existed that you were responsible for a very dreadful crime, but where legal proof was lacking. That would be an appalling event, which I would do my utmost to prevent. Think of the moral corruption and destruction that would inevitably attend a man if he became aware of his guilt, and that the state was unable to pursue him.

'You speak in a statement of yours of atonement for what you felt to be an offence against the moral law. You thought, naturally, of a moral atonement. What moral atonement could you think of, to a woman who had lost her life through your agency? Such things alarm me, and fill me with dread … Molenaar, my friend, do you also profit from our discussions?'

'Haven't heard a word, sir,' grunted the state policeman.

'Perhaps that is as well. I talk great heresy sometimes.'

'Come on,' grunted the butler.

Downstairs, once Martin was safely in his cubby-hole, the butler confided in another paperface in over-polished boots. 'Damn if I don't think old Bruin talks to his reflection while he shaves. Always damn speeches about morality – proper dominie he is, in church on a Sunday.' Quite a long speech from Mr Molenaar – perhaps he was getting the habit.

'This, remember, is entirely and strictly confidential. Only the report I make, finally, will be sent to the Officer of Justice, and then for his eyes only. Nobody at all hears what you say to me.'

The doctor was a tall pale man, strongly built and broad shouldered. He had a pale glossy face, and funny teeth; they were strong and white, but edged with gold and seemed badly arranged; he spoke like Winston Churchill on this account. He sat carefully behind his desk, well scrubbed and sterilized, with his big hairy hands folded across an exuberant stomach. He looked like a mighty beer drinker. He was a wooden Haarlemmer rather; his name was Professor Comenius.

Being a wooden Haarlemmer made him at first rather heavy-handed with Martin, humourless and inflexible. He warmed up, though. He had no real mannerisms, except fiddling with his expensive Sheaffer pen; his breast pocket was full of coloured Biros and pencils, but it was with this pen that he made notes, in a florid, broad-nibbed handwriting. He did not doodle, but his hands on his stomach twirled and twiddled the pen gently, between notes. Light filtered through white blinds, bounced off the silver cap of the Sheaffer, and off the gold teeth of Professor Comenius.

He neither smoked nor offered cigarettes to Martin, who had to roll his own; there was no objection. He was expert with shag by now, and could do it without looking. Professor Comenius watched everything with slightly protuberant, healthy lobster eyes.

Martin had been all set for enjoyable tests and games. He had greatly looked forward to Rorschach perhaps, or even an electro-encephalograph, but there had been no such toys; gadgets were out, in this place. He had been given a very thorough physical examination, followed by a series of routine questions like those on life insurance proposals. Had he ever suffered from tuberculosis – syphilis – epilepsy? Any head injuries? History of visible scars. War history, and military service. Birth, upbringing, growth, childhood illnesses, education. Parents, brothers, sisters. If dead what of? Employment; where, who, how long, why? It went on a good deal. The young doctor asking the questions talked with commas everywhere, as though he had worked for Harold Ross. He wrote the answers in neat tiny writing, and ran over the plainly inadequate spaces on the long, closely printed form. Martin tried to read upside down, but did not get far.

The state police had brought him early that morning, and again in the afternoon, but had not hung about; he was safely under the eye, here. More physical examination: eyes, ears, reflexes. He had been listened to, and tapped with hard fingers, been made to do balancing acts, and several tricks with eyes shut. 'Reach out and pick the matchbox off the table.' He had been very bad at this, he thought, and complained at the difficulty.

'You should see what they do for K.L.M. staff,' said one of the doctors, friendly. 'Always thinking up new tests for key personnel, far worse than these.'

Fluoroscope; he was screened with horrid chilly fingers putting his hands on his hips and pulling his shoulders back, while the cold metal was moved to touch his back. 'Deep breath in; hold it – two, three – that's it, get dressed.'

More queries, with a mental slant. Sleep well? Memory good? Happy in your work? Any trouble with your wife? Wife's relations? Inclined to nervous fatigue? Any difficulty in concentration? Accident prone at all? Any dislike of crowds? Of strangers? Any travel nervousness? Get on with your fellow workers? Their little mannerisms irritate you? An inordinate amount of blahblah.

And now he was with the big white chief, who had unbent enough by this time to make a few wooden Haarlemmer jokes. He had begun on Elsa, and was asking a great many questions about her. When Martin volunteered any information or tended towards monologue he was shut up sharply. But after an hour he felt relaxed and calm. This was a friendly enough old geyser; he was enjoying a pleasant euphoria.

Comenius lapsed into silence; for ten minutes he read his notes, adding a word here and there, not looking at Martin; he seemed to have forgotten his presence in analysing and adding up the score. 'Is it finished?' thought Martin, regretting the black leather couch and the pentothal, the voice telling him hypnotically to travel far back. 'I should enjoy that; invent all sorts of obscenities.'

Suddenly the psychiatrist started to speak again, still not looking at him, rapidly and abruptly, in a sharp challenging voice. In thirty seconds Martin's feeling of lazy contentment was far away. The friendly old geyser was far away too; a very tough personage had appeared in his place. Martin knew himself in the hands of a professional, able to demolish him with words. The acid voice never hesitated, never relaxed its grip, never allowed Martin any respite. The questions were pitiless and pointed.

'Were you angry ... were you glad ... did you realize ... don't talk, keep your answers brief ... don't become impatient it gets you nowhere ... how long ... how often ... if you had the chance ... were you violent ... stop ... when you were in the house ... how soon was that after ... was that immediately ... what did you say ... did you stop to think ... did that give you pleasure ... what was your reaction ... stop ... don't make a speech ... go forward to the time that ... and then ... were you frightened ... was there an argument ... who told you that ... why was it that ... why did you ... did you regret ... don't describe, simply relate ... was it painful ... what did she say ... was her face ... how much time ... was it the same ... on the other occasion ... longer or shorter ... of course you remember ... stop ... think ... concentrate on what you are saying ... that is irrelevant ... her clothes ... her eyes ... what sounds ... go back again to when ... don't interrupt ... don't invent ... give me an example ... be brief, be brief ... was that characteristic ... did it make a difference to your feelings ... that is meaningless ... define that more sharply ... that does not accord ... what do you say ... what colour ... stop ... don't give reasons ... once again do not be impatient, there is no need for tension, listen attentively and reply concisely.'

It went on for two hours or more. Martin's mind went round

flaring and sparking like a Catherine-wheel. He had no time to smoke a cigarette; had been told sharply not to fidget. It was much more like a criminal investigation than anything the magistrate had thrown at him, though the technique was similar; soften him up into relaxing his carefully planted guards and reflexes, then throw. This was a fast pitcher; the other had a most deceptive slow curve. He had the same sensation with both; the highly trained professional questioner, with skill in reaching essentials.

The doctor did not mention love, though he seemed able to gauge an emotional involvement in millimetres; how did he make love, how often, in what way, how long did it take? When at last the pressure lifted his shirt was soaking; under his arms, at his belt, between his shoulders. He felt bruised and aching all over, and said so. For the first time in a longish while Professor Comenius smiled.

'That is a common nervous reaction. Your mental equipment is lazy, and unused to strenuous exercise. I had to force you not to wind up your words in a jungle of irrelevant comparisons and qualifications; these are simply a cushion your mind lies on. You wished to – I will not say cheat – but fall soft. Your mind is, besides, very stiff and rigid, though not slow. Your nerve ends are reflecting unaccustomed use. We have finished. I hope to let the examining magistrate have any conclusions at the latest on the second day from now. You have been helpful and frank, which simplifies the task. Now I must make some details clear.

'Firstly, as you were told before we began, this has been and will remain confidential. I say this again because you were taken down on tape. Had I mentioned the existence of the recorder before, it would, very likely, have inhibited your ability to reply. You would have become hesitant, cautious and frightened. Now this tape is absolutely non-evidential in a legal sense. You were under no oath; it is strictly an exchange between doctor and patient; a verbal exchange. After my analysis of it is finished the tape is cleaned; the recording will

155

no longer exist. Is that clear? Nobody but myself has access to it; no word of our remarks goes outside the walls of this office, which is a private office in the sense that nobody enters it except in my presence. You may feel certain that no word reaches another ear. I wish you to feel able to accept that unreservedly.'

Feeling very tired, Martin nodded slowly.

'Second and last. The findings from this and the other examinations are not in any manner conclusive. They throw light upon your state of mind and upon the accuracy of your observation and description. They have nothing to do with responsibility for any action. If the examining magistrate makes use of them it is to clarify his ideas and no more. Should any process against you in the courts be begun as a result they are not evidence of anything at all.

'In short,' said Professor Comenius, putting his fingertips together and delivering what was probably a well-worn aphorism, 'this has been a quick cure. Exactly as if you had been on orange juice only for twenty-four hours to stimulate your physical processes, so this has been, mainly, a temporary stimulus to your nervous and mental functions. Try and profit by it to acquire a habit of clear and energetic thought.' He leaned over and pressed a bell on his desk. 'Communicate with the authorities, Dijkman, and inform them that we are ready.'

An anonymous person in a white coat left Martin to wait for half an hour before the boys in blue strolled in. There were a few words, a signature on a form, and they drove boredly back to the House of Keeping. The library man had been in, and left two fresh books on Martin's table. He was very tired, and flopped on his mattress; it was still too early for this officially, but nobody took any notice.

One was a dud, an English historical novel full of inns and gadzooks, but the other was a Simenon, one that he did not know. It was about a psychopath killer; Martin had finished it by ten o'clock, getting more frightened every minute.

He slept badly, turning, aching, itching, feeling hungry and sick alternately. He could not even smoke, and heard clocks strike four before he fell at last into the heavy delayed sleep of over-exhaustion. It was worse when he woke. He tried to work, but *cafard* gnawed at him increasingly. The smell of soap made him want to vomit; there was no air in the overheated cell. Had Van der Valk found anything at all that really did point to another person? Wasn't it quite likely that all that photographic stuff was just a lot of hooey? Mightn't the whole affair be an elaborate farce, intended to put him off his guard, to give him false confidence? It would be just like the pack of them. They had no proof; they would wait for him to give it them.

They were waiting for his nerve to give way, till he could no longer keep it to himself. Van der Valk had said that the magistrate knew how to get the truth out of him. It all added up to the fact that they were going to turn the screw till he broke. That terrible man with the gold teeth. 'Nothing to do with responsibility.' A singularly uninformative remark. He would minute: 'This man is not insane.' Or would he? Would the minute read: 'Clearly insane. Committed the crime, but has no present recollection of having done so?'

The magistrate, with his polite, veiled hints. 'Moral corruption and destruction' – We will hound you increasingly, till you confess, and expiate. Their chain of circumstantial evidence that was insufficient; they would wait for their case to become incontestable. If he was insane they would move him into a clinic; give him another team of headshrinkers to play with. No, he was sane, and holding out, hiding guilty knowledge, cleverly so far, but he could not keep it up. He would vomit it all out; they knew how to break his hold. 'You may feel that morally you are responsible. An appalling situation which I will do my utmost to prevent. We have no legal proof. You, *jongen,* are going to give us that proof, get it?'

They were all so bloody gentle and kind and sympathetic,

the bastards. A polite menace, a torture *à la chansonette*. 'Say what you know; it makes it easier for you. Don't imagine; think.' Moral atonement. What was that? Not suicide; that was an act of despair. Not the guillotine, here. To sit, a lifetime, in prison up in Leeuwarden with the cyanide doctor and the other murderers? To confess, first? Acquire the habit of clear and energetic thought.

With an effort he said – 'You're not thinking now; this is certainly a fantasy. Start again, thinking clearly and avoiding fantasy.' You will know the truth. Did you then kill her? Was your story the truth, yes, exact, but with a little tiny piece left out? You rang the doorbell, yes? *En toen?* You rang; she answered, you talked, she talked; you wished to make love. It was on this occasion, not the other, that you were impotent, eh, and suddenly impatience gave way to despairing fury, of a man enslaved, humiliated, and now, finally, castrated, and that was the end of the line. You went, for you knew, to where the gun was kept, and waited till realization put terror in her eyes, and then you shot the witch four times in the belly.

Yes, yes, with silver bullets, no doubt. Goddam fantasy again. All that was absolute rubbish. Slipping, though, got to take steps. Discipline. How does one do this? Prayers. Can't remember any prayers, but got to clear my head. If you can't do the job you must get help. God is there, huh? Yes, I know; you only say prayers when you are frightened. Last time was in the war, telling yourself that you don't hear the one that hits you. First the bang and then that short wheep, that tells you it's eighty-eight. Now stop that, and put yourself on the floor on your knees. *Merde,* burned it, floor bit my knee. If a bullet comes, God, let it be somewhere that gives me a few seconds to say act of contrition, and not blinded, please, God, nor castrated. Dead if you like, that's what I'm for. But don't tell the man over there with the Spandau. Oh, in heaven's name, control your imagination, boy.

He said prayers. He said 'Our Fathers', slowly.

'Hold your breath, and say one; say three before you light

another cigarette. And think what you are saying.' The whole day spread around him full of horrors that pressed in with nasty clammy hands. They threatened him till a dozen times that day he wept and whined; yes, he had killed her, but leave me now in peace. In his lucid moments he told himself angrily not to be such a fool. 'Don't be a fool; you're not only a fool, *sufferd, klootzak*. Don't you know any other languages? Insults, at least, in Spanish. Or in Italian. Yes. *Stronzo, pirla, froggio, finocchio, osso buco, gazo, fica. Menos male; va.'*

He had a need for fresh air, to feel the damp wind on his face and set his feet to a pavement with rain on it. Listen if there is a boat, there in the Amstel, tooting for the Sarphati bridge to swing for her, creeping up into the heart of the town, her gentle wake swishing against the quay by Carré. The other side of this water is the Stadhouderskade, going up towards the Leidseplein, Elsa's favourite walk. Two minutes' walk across that water, in the tangle of old-fashioned streets around the Vermeerplein, just before you reach the screaming traffic of the Van Baerlestraat, lies the Matthew Maris.

That evening, telling the story to Van der Valk, had opened old wounds in Martin. Of love and hate and enslavement. Like her little donkey he had been. Carrying her shopping bag. The waterway up to the Nassaukade, and the little shop by the Rozengracht bridge where she bought her cheese; the cheap butcher and the dear butcher, the wine shop in the Vermeerstraat, the cigar shop and the cleaners, the ironmonger, Albert Heijn and De Gruyter and Simon de Wit – the whole neighbourhood had known what he was, running to the chemist every month for large neat anonymous packets. The things you do when young and in love, thinking that nobody else in the world feels the way you do.

Even now, ten years afterwards, he would not have bought as much as a packet of cigarettes in the whole neighbourhood, for fear of the little flicker of recognition in a shopkeeper's eye.

How young he had been, and how ridiculously immature, wilfully doing incredible things to *épater le bourgeois*. Amsterdammers are not so easily scandalized. And there are so many other young men with noisy and childish tastes.

She had hated the Matthew Maris. Achterbuurt, she had called it, slummy district, quite unfairly. Dreadfully she had envied Toon, who was successful and well off, and lived in the flossy quarter down by the Beatrix Park. She had wanted to live looking at the water. Well she had made it. The Josef Israels might not be a dream of luxury, but at least it was in Amsterdam-Zuid, and looking at the water. How she had cursed when the children screamed, playing in the narrow street, so that the sound echoed between the tall houses: might as well live in the Jordaan, she said. She despised the heavy, rather ugly, but solid, dignified Museumplein district. But at least through those thick walls you did not hear the neighbours scratching themselves. Just as well, he thought with a grin, remembering whimsicalities of passion. The roses he had had to pick with his teeth. Love under the shower; love on the kitchen table; love in Amsterdam. He had thought that love was like that; the memory gave him little pleasure.

Stop the goddam stream of consciousness, idiot, think. Say more prayers. Wasn't easy, hadn't been to Mass for twelve years or more. Couldn't remember further than 'Judge me O God' – disconcerting – and 'I will wash my hands among the innocent' – hardly helpful. Wouldn't do. *'Credo in unum Deum'*; that was better, I believe in one God. Big blank, something about Pontius Pilate – whom he had always thought rather unlucky, doing his best to manœuvre in a decidedly slippery situation – until one came near the end.

'Credo in unam, sanctam, catholicam ecclesiam.' Didn't sound right. Latin adjectives, forgotten, never been any good at them anyway. Word missing, somehow, too. Try and remember. Think of Maria Laach, and the monks tossing phrases from one side of the choir to the other, a shower of golden balls. Embroidered notes like old manuscripts, blocky

Gothic capitals turning into gay birds and flowers. Got it. *Unam sanctam* – or was it -um – came on one side, and the other chirped straight in; *apostolicam ecclesiam*.

And then there was something about one baptism and the remission of sins. Not a very efficient prayer.

He realized that he was in the grip of neurosis and made a considerable effort. He lit a cigarette and sat cross-legged on the floor. A slight temporary neurosis, induced by psychiatric gobbledygook, and the strain of uncertainty. Compensations, or adjustments, or whatever, had got bumped a bit loose. These were all symptoms – that feeling that people were trapping him was simply schizophrenic. And this ridiculous idea of being a black-out killer, a common delusion; the old legend of the *Doppelganger,* the alternate self who did wicked things. Now get into bed and behave sensibly. You did not kill her, so don't go running to claim punishment, just to purge a feeling of guilt.

Same old story, always wanting to add to one's self-importance. Every time there is a murder a heap of lunatics run to the police station with elaborate, ingenious, totally imaginary confessions. He fell asleep thinking of his army chaplain, a young Belgian Jesuit who grinned when the others called him *cocu,* and fitted his own words out of psalms to the songs about Angeline, where every line had to rhyme with *'encule'*. But not even the Germans could sing like our mob.

The minibus again, the familiar mousehole, the only-too-familiar face of Mr Molenaar, who made a smile of acquaintanceship if not pleasure. He said good morning, but like a man who is not too sure. The delightful office of Mr Slotemaker de Bruin, rather darkened by the weather. It was a vile day with sleet in front of a high wind, and he had his reading lamp on. Today he had a dark reddish suit with faint green lines in it, and an apricot tie. He did not look in the least like a public prosecutor – was that a good omen? His eyes had a strong greenish glint. He began without preamble.

'I have had the report from the clinic, from Professor Comenius. He finds no doubt in your statements, and no reason to throw doubt upon them. He describes you as lucid and with some gift for expressing yourself. You are inclined to be diffuse and verbose, and to be overlong in coming to the point. Mm, rather like some officers of justice. However, he thinks you both an observant and an accurate witness, as they go, and that – where am I? – your view of matters is not more than normally distorted by your individual vision. For a psychiatrist, he is unusually complimentary. That's all he says that need concern you; his report is, naturally, confidential.

'There is little to be added; I have given this matter a lot of thought. I am instructing the authorities concerned that I do not believe the interests of justice to be furthered by holding you any longer in custody.'

Martin, absurdly, was trying to recall an obscene rhyme of his childhood, chanted by dirty little boys, beginning *'Un jour un charcutier, en découpant de l'andouille ...'* but he could only remember the last line: *'Des affaires du cul je ne m'en occupe plus.'* It seemed to fit the situation; he felt a childish reprieve from care.

The communicating door opened and a typist came in, a fat, middle-aged woman with a stenographer's brisk fingers. She was considerably corseted, had a neat black suit and an unsuitable blouse, and her kind bun of a face was unpainted, creased with fine confidential wrinkles. She murmured.

'Very well,' said the magistrate. 'My regrets, and I will not keep him waiting long; indeed on second thoughts he need not wait at all. Ask him to be good enough to come in.'

She waddled out comfortably, and a moment later Van der Valk's untidy face appeared in the doorway. Martin waited with some amusement to see whether the magistrate altered his verbal style with policemen.

'My dear inspector, good morning. Do me the pleasure of sitting down. I asked for you to give me a little time; I am not satisfied that our friend here is answerable for this affair of the unfortunate de Charmoy. I have informed him that I propose to order his provisional release; he understands, naturally, that he is unreservedly available to you should the need arise, as a witness. Now I wish to benefit from your conclusions; you may indeed have made new discoveries. The investigation had better proceed on a new premise, with my confidence and support, be it added.'

Van der Valk did not look at Martin; his voice was level. 'We have more than a basic premise; I am glad to say that we have a very promising line of inquiry, which I wish to report, Sir.'

'That is encouraging. A moment,' he turned to Martin. 'I am pleased that your confidence has been rewarded. I hope that it will not prove necessary to bring you here again. I am pleased to have made your acquaintance. Molenaar, perhaps you would let our friend wait till I can have a word with the director of the House of Keeping.'

Outside, the state policeman showed Martin a thin smile. 'Slid out, then. Good luck.'

'Nice knowing you all, but I can't say I'll be sorry,' grinned Martin.

Three hours later, his weekend bag over his shoulder, he was struggling against a fierce gusting wind up towards the Marnixstraat. The windows of the Haarlem bus were blurred by streaming rain; scurrying passers-by were whirled like leaves across the open spaces; hats went into the air like the larks ascending. A pompous woman had her umbrella blown inside out, and was rude to the conductor, who, quite likely on purpose, overshot her stop in Halfweg. The water of the Amsterdamse Vaart was shaking itself and rattling at the canal banks like a bored child in a play-pen.

Another hour, and he was drinking coffee in his own living-room, with Sophia fussing over him slightly.

'First I'll go out and buy an enormous steak, and I'll make Béarnaise; is that a good idea?'

'Very good.'

He sat like a sultan reading weekly papers, ate happily through the enormous steak, went back to his papers while she washed up, and was half asleep by the time she came back, changed and bringing tea and chocolate.

'We've a bottle of marc; I'll get it first, and then tell you what's been happening to me.'

After he had seen her last, at the Palais de Justice the day he went into the House of Keeping, Sophia, rather tempted to cry, had sat a few minutes to finish her cigarette. Van der Valk had disappeared, and she was taken aback when he accosted her on the pavement outside.

'I'll give you a lift if I may.' She got into the Volkswagen and he moved off into the traffic, but on the car park off the Marnixstraat, where the Haarlem bus waits, he stopped the car and turned the engine off.

'Look, I want to talk a little; is that allowed?'

'Go on.'

'Are you in a hurry? I can drive you to Haarlem, or I could come back this evening if you'd prefer.'

'I'm not in a hurry now, and I'll have plenty to do this evening.'

'Very well. I'm pretty sure that your husband didn't kill anybody. I am also pretty confident that the examining magistrate will come to the same conclusion. May take him a few days. This is quite straightforwardly a manœuvre to gain time. I have no proof of anything, but I do possess at this moment a strong piece of indirect evidence. Now I don't want you to go thinking that your husband is being victimized, and tearing off to lawyers, and imagining that I am suppressing this evidence. You had some such idea, didn't you?'

'Yes, I did.'

'Would it put your mind at rest if I told you what I have?'

'I think I have a right to know, don't you think?'

'I think you do at that, but I hesitate to show you this; it is a rather horrible business.'

'Much more horrible for me if my husband were to go on trial for a murder he did not do.'

He studied her face a moment and nodded, putting his hand in his pocket. The envelopes that Martin had seen were gone, and the twenty or so photos that he handed her had been wrapped in tissue and tucked into an old wallet. She unwrapped them slowly and studied them one by one. Van der Valk watched her wooden face with some curiosity. When she had seen them all she went through them again, before folding the tissue again and handing them back.

They were of Elsa, all of them; Elsa wearing a black mask but quite naked. The first dozen were simply a series of poses, lovely, lewd and intricate. They had been taken in her living-room, carefully lit and photographed with great expertise and a good deal of artistic sense. Her hair had been skilfully arranged and her body composed to heighten the effect.

The others were different. Still highly artistic; good composition and technically extremely proficient. They had been taken by remote control. Elsa wore the mask again; her smile in close-up was almost a rictus, and sweat was showing alongside her nose. The man's head had been masked by a black hood; Ku-Klux stuff. These pictures were of a careful, studied obscenity that was most effective; the last few were staggering.

Sophia gave Van der Valk a slightly malicious smile.

'They will look fine on your office wall.'

He grinned back, relieved. 'I've shown them to no one yet but the chief inspector.'

'And what did he say?'

'Nothing. Spilt his coffee down his shirt. We get a few of these, you know, but they're not often of this standard. Pretty talented – not hack work. And a model who knows and enjoys her work – that's rare too.' His voice was not malicious.

'So there is a man, and that is his picture – up to a point.'

'Yes. And he must be lying very low. He can't know whether we've found these. Fears it. He'll be sweating in his socks. But so long as your husband's in jail he will think himself safe.

165

Get it, now? He'll do a lot to get these back. Tricky situation, though. He may not dare try and break into the flat, for fear of failing, and letting us know he's failed. Nothing been tried yet; he might not know where she hid them. He's wide awake, and tense – good thing that; makes him give it away the easier. But a breath of an idea that we're after him and he's vanished. We don't know his face. We might find a likely bloke, but we'd have to bring him in and say, "All right you, take your clothes off and try this for size; sorry, we haven't a woman handy." I hope I don't offend you.

'I incline to think this is a racket; woman's mask is just an added excitement, common prop in pornography, but the man's mask is a disguise; maybe he was thinking of marketing these. Makes good money; you need a safe outlet. Camera, book and antique shops, and so on.'

'This must be someone recent in her life, surely? Otherwise you'd have found a trace of some kind, I should have thought.'

'That's it. Entirely new character. Look, if I may I'll call on you in Haarlem tomorrow night. I hope I've relieved your mind. Your husband won't come to any harm in jail, and he won't stay there long. Like me to drive you home?'

He was as good as his word, and back the next evening. Sophia made him coffee, and gave him a large gin.

'People would say I suspected you, or was trying to make you,' with content, leaning back and crossing his legs.

She gave herself a small gin, sitting upright. 'Why have you come, tell me.'

'Helps, you know, to talk to an interested person. Seldom possible. Helps thought; helps unwind.'

'What about your wife?'

'Rule number one; never talk shop at home. My wife is bored and disgusted with police work. In this case, you're not. And you're in a peculiar position. I pulled a fast one on your husband, maybe, and feel the need to justify myself. And you know more or less about the whole business.'

'More or less? I know nothing at all. I am not interested in

Elsa de Charmoy; I detested her, but I don't want to cross-examine my husband; what he tells me will be fragmentary. You can let him go tomorrow, without a thing against him; he will still have sat in jail, under suspicion of killing a woman he once loved. I get a slight idea that you are holding me under observation; is that so?'

'Yes, up to a point.'

'Mm. I am more likely, certainly, to have murdered her than my husband. Still, assume, for the present that I did not murder her, and know nothing about it. That I have never been in the house on the Josef Israelskade. Will you tell me the story?'

Van der Valk told the story, concise, clear and fluent. Sophia listened without interruption. She poured another cup of coffee.

'And now what?'

'Not very easy to say. Two classic methods. One is to go very quietly, putting nets down and dragging them till you get a shark inside. The other is to make a great noise, arresting people – or saying you have – all over the place, policemen poking round everywhere dressed as gas-meter men, saying how interested they've always been in photographs of naked women; has anyone some to spare? Idea is to make your man nervous, lose his head, run. Tips his hand. Popular method, because people do silly things and it shows them up. Not so good in this case, because I think he's all set to run anyway. No clue to his identity; everybody carries cameras; no law against it.

'No; in this instance we sink the nets and start sweeping quietly. For instance, might be a professional photographer, huh? So far, I've turned up every professional between Den Helder and Amersfoort. Hell of a lot there are too. Likeliest he lives right here in Amsterdam, but it could be Noordwijk or Uitgeest for all we know.'

'But surely he lives near the Josef Israels, don't you think?'

'Why so definite?'

'I don't know, it was instinctive.'

'Try and see why.'

'Yes; you said that nobody had noticed a stranger in the district, first; that strikes me as queer. The old woman, the other neighbours, the police. Even if he only came at night, I should think that someone would have an impression of a strange face, a strange car, something. Isn't it logical to suppose that he isn't a stranger at all? Lives maybe right there in the street?'

'Go on with that idea.'

'There isn't any more. But now that I think of it, none of her friends had any idea that she was running round with anybody new – isn't that right?'

'Yes, and a puzzling thing, that. Pointed to someone out of the past. Your husband fitted exactly – too exactly for me.'

'Well, if you meet someone new, your friends do too as a rule. They see him in your house and you likely take him along to theirs. Someone surely would have seen him. So unlikely, somehow.'

'Go on. This interests me.'

'She moved in a narrow little world, like all of us, come to that – except policemen. I can't see her just picking him up in the street or in a café. Wouldn't it make sense if it was somebody local, whom she could have met in a shop, or in front of her own doorstep? Someone whom the old woman, for example, might know but wouldn't notice, just because he walks down the street every day to get the tram. Does it make sense to you?'

Van der Valk finished his cold coffee.

'Woman's explanation, but anyway an explanation of something that bothers me, and has since I began this. I don't altogether like it, but it's given me an idea.' He put a cigarette in his mouth and pointed at her with the matchbox. 'Mousetrap. Police technique from time of Noah, modernized by Gestapo.'

'Huh?'

'Look, we comb camera shops and so on, but nothing we

can go on helps us much. The photos, technically, are common stuff, ordinary paper, Gevaert film, camera a miniature, Leica or Contax – just as likely Japanese, nowadays. The arc-lamps in the flat may have been hers, but anyway they come from a manufacturer that sells them by the hundred. All very vague. So I get an idea based on your supposition. A mouse-trap is a cine-camera, wide-angle, telescopic lens, blahblah; we put it in the Josef Israels, with a man who knows how to use it. Get a few feet of interesting passers-by, and make a little documentary of the habits of the street. You can learn anything about a place this way. Two disadvantages: lengthy and expensive. But it might be worth trying.'

Sophia drank some gin and rocked her glass gently, making patterns with the droplets. 'Still a bit dubious about me?'

Van der Valk pulled at his lip and rubbed his nose; Martin would have recognized that he was dubious. 'It would be a lot easier, wouldn't it? I can't say I like the notion of fishing round half Amsterdam for a man when I don't even know what he looks like. All the people packed into houses round there between the Mauvestraat and the Lutmastraat, and again across the canal; he could live anywhere there. At the same time one thing helps; he will be interested in the Josef Israels, and I think he'll be keeping an eye on it, because of the photos. He'll want to know whether we've found them; they were well hidden. Anyway,' he got up, 'thank you for the idea.'

'You're welcome,' said Sophia gravely.

'That's quite a few days ago now; I haven't seen him since,' said Sophia, breaking chocolate with a loud snap.

'Mm; I saw him this morning in the magistrate's office, but didn't speak with him of course. He said that he'd a lead of some description. Must have, or he wouldn't have gone to the magistrate. Unless he'd heard that I was to be released anyway. Spoil his cover. The idea was to keep me in jail till they knew something about these pictures. I don't know; I got shuffled out quick; confidential reports and so on.'

At that moment the bell rang, a bossy pip-pip.

'That's police, you can bet your life.'

It was; like an actor on cue Van der Valk walked in, all smiles and congratulations.

'What a pleasure,' grinned Martin, 'to sit on a comfortable chair when I talk to you.'

'I didn't only come for laughs all the same; something important to tell you.'

'You like marc?'

'Don't know, what is it?'

'Here. And here's to you. You said you'd get me out and you did, too.'

'Good,' said Van der Valk, tasting. 'No, he let you go quite off his own bat, apart from anything I had to say. As you saw, I had a session with his nibs today. He let you go, right; he would have given that to the Press. I had to stop that in a hurry, and to do that I had to show my hand. Luckily it's fairly strong by now. The pictures for a start; you should have seen him. Took them over to the window to get a good light, laughed heartily, and then said in the nastiest voice he has, "If I have the prosecuting of this individual he will wish he hadn't been born." You've only seen his bedside manner; you ought to see him with his robes on in court. Frightens even me, believe me.'

'These photos,' said Martin plaintively, 'they sound like hotsy-totsy; can't I get to see them now everybody else has had a good laugh?'

'Haven't got them any more; he kept them. We've copies but they're in the office. And' – in his ferocious voice – 'you're the boy who has seen the beauty take her knickers off anyway.' Martin was squashed by Sophia's sarcastic smile.

'However,' the other went on, 'since Madame here gave me the idea, and you're involved in this now, I'm going to tell you something which is police business. I did what I was thinking of, and put a camera in the Josef Israels. Seemed a good joke, to try and catch the candid cameraman with our own version. Well, yesterday the operator got an interesting bit of footage.

'Man comes over the wooden bridge from the Waalstraat, looks up at the house a second, and does a double-take; we got it too. He looks again with something of a stare, as though something had changed and caught his eye, and it were important enough to stop him in his tracks, which it did, only for a second.

'Now plenty of people stare, because the street was named in the paper – but not the actual house. So the curious and the nasty-minded stare at the row of houses – "Oo, in one of those there's been 'orrible murder!" They have their mouths open.' He gave an imitation of a morbid sightseer. 'This chap is different; lucky I had an intelligent fellow behind the camera. He got it all, good and clear, dead in focus. Catches the expression nicely. It's a strange expression; expectant, excited almost.

'You see, to film we pulled up the Venetian blind. They'd been lowered ever since the day, and were up for the first time. Now that isn't a thing that strikes the ordinary passer-by. What does he know or care whether the *jalousies* are up or down? But the character we have in mind has been keeping a sharpish eye on this house and he would rumble the difference at once. He would think we were searching again, because of course the camera's not visible from the street.

'It wasn't long; he gave a quick, sharp look, standing stock-still for a second, started to move, hesitated a moment and then just walked away down the street, smartish. Anyway I thought it time to test your theory a little, Madame, and I had stills made from the film and tried them on the old woman. They're clear – I'll show you – we have him full face, profile and back. And she came in handy in the end, the old bitch. She says she's seen him often, and he does in fact – exactly as you suggested – go along the quay every morning, whether to cross the Amstel or up Van Woustraat is of little consequence. I don't know where he works – not a camera shop by the way at least, because we've checked every one in the town.

'I'm not certain, but I have an impression he took fright. He's not so stupid, this one. He may have had ideas of breaking into the house, but certainly wouldn't dare now, so it's no use doing anything corny like sitting in the dark waiting for a visitor. He may not have known where she hid the pictures, may not even have expected her to have kept them – what I mean is that it would accord with her character to have told him they'd been destroyed. He may be gambling on our not having found them and not looking for what we don't know exists.

'Today he doesn't show for the camera; that doesn't mean much. I should like to know where he lives, but I haven't the men to go nosing in every corner; we aren't the F.B.I. with a thousand judo experts and television hidden in a baker's van. Not having all this tripe means we have to use our brains, though. The magistrate agrees that there's nothing to be done for the moment; he likes the stills, but says rightly that they're inconclusive. If we find him tomorrow on this route, I'm thinking of turning on the pressure a little to see if he gets rattled. Trouble is to get something conclusive. Can't compare the photo with the witches' sabbath in the mask because while they're the same height and build so are a good few million others. Anyway, clothes change a figure considerably. We want something to tie him to Elsa, or to the naughty pictures; these stills aren't evidence of anything. So he walked in the street and looked at a house. Annoying situation.

'Look, *jongen,* I want you to stay here at home and keep quiet; that's what I came to tell you. I say I want; in fact it's an order, get it? No paper, officially, knows you've been released, but they've a right to publish the fact if they find out. We would be shown up, wanting to conceal things, and we might as well say straight out that we have fresh evidence. If anyone drops around and finds you drinking gin in comfort instead of that Government coffee in the Weteringschans, then our friend will know, and if I should have pinpointed the wrong fellow then I've balled up the whole business, and deserve every word the magistrate says.'

Van der Valk finished his long monologue in a stand-no-nonsense voice and blew a fan of smoke at the ceiling. Martin watched him stolidly.

'Do you think it possible that the cameraman knows me? By sight, I mean?'

'Yes, of course he does.'

'How d'you establish that so certainly? We don't know that he ever laid eyes on me. You don't even know why Elsa was killed. Looked as though it were something to do with me; I agonized over that a good deal in jail, but now I incline to see my connexion with this as pure coincidence.'

'Yap, coincidence,' tartly. 'It's part of the same pattern. Sure, I don't know exactly why she was killed at that moment, though I've a good guess, but I don't care. The pattern would lead eventually to violence, it's in her character. You threw a hot-water bottle; sooner or later someone would throw a bullet. As for his knowing you – have you forgotten how I picked you up so fast in the first place?'

'The photo of me in the Kalverstraat.'

'Taken in the street, we'll never know how, perhaps, but to me it's easy. She was in the street with boyfriend, and saw you. On a sudden impulse – "Snap that man there staring in the window." He had his little camera, and liked that kind of trick. Carry it further; say she never told him who it was – one of her little mysteries – and put it in her bureau. He took it and developed it, and he had maybe kept a copy.

'Now follow me; one night he's with her, making love, and there's been a row. She loved rows, intrigues, jealousies – heightened the tension. Side by side with the need for sex, too, she has the need to lie and mystify – it's the pivot of her character. Suddenly the bell rings. Don't answer. You down there step into the street and look up towards the window, just like everybody when the bell doesn't answer.

'Now suppose he, not she, stepped through the curtain to see

173

who the late visitor is, especially since visitors haven't been encouraged lately. Quite plainly, in the light of the street, he recognized your face, just as the policeman recognized it from the same photo. This is a coincidence, if you like, but it's basic; the whole thing turns on it, to my thinking. You're in the same sort of attitude as in the Kalverstraat. "That man; they know each other; he knows where she lives and comes late at night." Possessive, he thinks that's just for one thing, knowing Elsa's little ways. Jealousy and rage flare up like petrol; he lost his control and ran to the writing desk; the gun was kept there openly, in a cigar-box. She may have run too, thinking he was after the photo; perhaps there was a struggle. He pushed hard, and gave her the business with the gun. In a smallish room, loud, convincing bang; gave him a fright. His head cleared; she's on the floor, knocked out, not even knowing what hit her, and he thinks she's dead. Boyfriend has read the books, knows what to do. *Verdorie,* dead woman — *alors* handkerchief, wipe the gun off, put it in her hand. She let it fall later, her prints smeared all over it. There was maybe a glass, a cup — wipe it all off, wipe everything he might have touched. It all takes five minutes or less. He's standing wondering if he's forgotten anything when she stirs, moans, maybe speaks. Not dead, possibly not even dangerously hurt if she's helped fast. But here you see boyfriend in a clear light. He bunks. He runs like hell, slams the door, takes the steps three at a time in sheer panic, and leaves her there to die.

'In the open air he has just enough grip to walk slowly; you might still be hanging about. But you don't know him; nobody knows him; he's her little secret. He goes to bed sweating, but he calms down, reflecting that nothing can really connect him with her, just provided the police don't find those pictures; they won't, they're too stupid. He feels quite safe when you're arrested. Better still, you can't give an explanation that satisfies us. He was right, he thinks; he was right; you are the one she was cheating him with; all right, he got the two of you. He's almost happy, bar the tiny seed of uneasiness over the photos, since the damn police keep floating about the house. Just keep an eye open till the heat cools off.'

Martin poured out another little glass of marc. Van der Valk drank it straight off.

'That's all fantasy, pure visualizing, irrelevant and unimportant. It was like that. The mechanics of the thing aren't important except that you couldn't understand how she was killed. He'll spill it all when we get him; that type's great on what they felt and what they thought. There's a difference in character there between him and you that is revealing; you felt only pity, even a recurrence of love when you saw her dead. That moment in the Binnen Gasthuis I could see clear as print you hadn't killed her. You're a hopeless liar.'

Sophia gave a small naughty snigger, causing Martin to look crossly at her.

'But him,' went on Van der Valk, missing the ashtray, 'he kept thinking of his injuries and grievances. He's a lot younger than you, of course; maybe twenty-three or four.'

'Let's have a look at the stills.' The policeman rustled in his briefcase and handed them over, half a dozen clear, sharp prints blown up to the size of a quarto page. Apart from one or two wavy blurs, caused perhaps by the window-pane, the definition was that of sight.

He looked carefully at the narrow, clever, rather handsome face staring with the oddly eager look up at the window. He wore no hat, and had fair wavy hair. The face was a little too narrow, the nose a little too sharp. The hands were in the pockets of the short raincoat. It was a distinctive face, young and attractive like a boy scout; alert, observant and a little humourless.

'And the bird knows me?'

'Yes.'

'So you're warning me to keep out of sight.'

'Yes.'

'My turn to have an idea.'

'Costs nothing, so far.'

'Assuming this is our pigeon. Sight of me gave him a considerable shock, and the result – bang! Sounds cracked but in context, the way you tell it, it hangs together.'

'Yes. Several things combined to pull the trigger; chain reaction. But seeing you sparked it off.'

'Seeing me sparked him off. Let's read it that instead of hiding here I wait in the street instead of your geyser, to pick him up. I follow him, openly, so that he sees me. If it's the wrong man, it doesn't affect him. Just another person, behaving in what seems an aimless way. But if it's the right man, the shock's considerable. Not only am I not in jail, but I know him, and am following him, for a vendetta or something. If it were me it would scare me blue. You want to throw him off balance, for a start. As for the link with Elsa, I'm linked to her, publicly, and by this bastard who shot her four times and left her to die on the floor. If I can shake this geyser down, needle him into talking, that completes the link. Maybe he'll try to hit me,' added Martin with enjoyment.

Van der Valk rubbed his nose furiously.

'What you propose is illegal, unethical and in short unpermissible.'

'So were a few of the things you did, buster. Examining magistrate talked a lot about ethics sacrificed to expediency. Suppressing that search and those photos too. Not to mention a raw deal here. You owe me something.'

'You trying to twist my arm or something?'

'Just wanting to stop being the big prat in the middle all the time. I haven't been particularly proud of my record so far. I'm sick of it. I want to go to war.'

'Stop talking so much, you're frightening me. If I allow you to do any damn thing at all it's only under my complete control. No question of your playing games. The idea is not too stupid. If I use you it's as a witness, that's all, get it? Instead of a witness *à décharge* you become *à charge*. Now you'll follow my instructions implicitly and that's flat. This is what I'm thinking of doing.' He thought for a while.

'If he comes to work in the morning – and if he doesn't I'll put the heat on the whole district – he passes the Van Wou-straat anyway. You wait there on the corner of the Josef Israels. I'll be behind, over the bridge to the Rijnstraat, in a black Mercedes with German plates. On the other side –' he glanced at Sophia – 'would you be willing to play this too? If I use one of you, I'd rather have you both.'

'Yes,' she said unemotionally.

'On the other side, then, you wait, Madame, and behind you is Inspector Wouwerman, that's our old pal Henk. If he walks, when and if he arrives, you all walk. If he rides, you take the tram with him. He'll stick to his ordinary routine, because any departure from the ordinary is just something more looking odd and possibly needing explanation . . . All right. You sit or stand near him, and if he catches your eye put on a bit of pres-sure; smile and say good morning. If he says, "Who are you, I don't know you," or something, just say you're sure you know his face, but don't push it; try not to talk. Don't cross the road; that's part of the point of having two; just keep parallel-ing the route.

'When he gets off the tram follow quietly, not too close, ten paces or so. If he stops or doubles back let him pass. If he just stops, stop too, and stare at him. If he tackles you, and asks why you're following him, then say, "I wanted to talk to you; let's have a little chat; come and have a drink." Go inside a café, don't stop on the terrace. I'll join you. If he tries to lose you by dodging about, don't fluster yourself. He might try some trick to shake you off, like flying into the Bijenkorf and out the far side, or jumping on a bus just before the doors shut. In that case, just hang on for me. I'm responsible for everything. If he gets angry, needle him if you like but don't get in a fight unnecessarily, even if you're anxious to poke him. Anyway Henk or I will be right there. When he goes in anywhere like a cigar shop or something simply wait outside. No F.B.I. stuff and no drama. I'm going now, and I'll work out details. Be at the bureau at seven in the morning, and I'll put you in the picture, that's if I decide to go through with this, because it's sufficiently screwy and the chief inspector wouldn't wear it. Understood?'

'I feel as though I were going to the guillotine.'

'Passes off,' said Sophia indifferently. 'Wanting to yawn all the time?'

'Yes, the English call it having the wind up.'

'Drive slowly.' It was pitch dark. The road was slightly icy, and Martin let the little Dauphine find its way gently. It was ten to seven when he parked in the Ferdinand Bolstraat. A black Mercedes with German plates was a little ahead, seventy or eighty yards from the bureau. He grinned at the depressed agent on duty in 'reception'.

'Van der Valk in?'

'Go ahead if you know the way.'

There were two or three cold and weary policemen warming themselves at the stove, longing for the shift to end. In his office Van der Valk was talking to a young *rechercheur* like a boxer, square and dark, with a dog's flat affectionate features and soft brown eyes.

'Wait a moment in the charge room.'

The big room with its untidy desks was occupied by a woman scrubbing; the wait seemed interminable. Several people came and went and paid no attention, and Martin glimpsed Henk, lugubrious and as though needing a shave. The stove was lit but not yet hot; grey light was crawling laboriously in through the window; it was all most depressing. Finally Van der Valk came in, wrapped in an overcoat, pale and underfed-looking.

'And –?' he asked. 'Still think it sounds clever?'

'Nothing else would have got me out at six on a morning like this.'

'Oh, to be a policeman; nothing out of the ordinary for me. All right, let's ride or we might miss the birdy.'

'Ride!' said Henk disgustedly. 'You ride; we get on the stink-

ing tram —good day too to fall in the canal. Oh, to be a policeman, and have a big Mercedes car with a heater, and get
happy music-while-you-work on the radio.'

'Two quick pips means here we come; two quick and a slow
like Victor Silvester means going the wrong way and I follow,'
said Van der Valk casually. 'Where the hell have I left my
gloves.'

Two or three other *rechercheurs* left with them, going in
different directions, swinging their legs up on to bicycles. The
boxer had a scruffy scooter. Henk had a Tyrolean hat and a
leather coat, like a German tourist. Walking along the Josef
Israelskade Martin had a strong wish to look up at the windows, which he stifled. He wondered whether the camera was
still quietly watching up there. His stomach felt nasty and he
wished he had a drink. He wore the same hat and raincoat he
had worn to visit Elsa. Twenty yards behind him, Sophia was
dressed as a secretary on her way to work, with a huge bag, a
sombre raincoat and a gay umbrella, and a scarf instead of a
hat. Three or four people were walking the same way by now
though it was still early, and a steady stream of bicycles was
crossing the bridge from the Rijnstraat.

At the tram stop Martin had plenty of time to stroll about
and get bored. The wait lasted a cigarette and a half and
three trams; he had almost forgotten to listen when he heard
the two toots; the Mercedes whined softly past and stopped a
couple of hundred yards further. A young man was walking
up the street towards Martin, wearing a short raincoat and
carrying a briefcase, like ten thousand others in Amsterdam
on a cold and disagreeable morning. But the sharp nose was
unmistakable. His steps rang unhurried on the pavement; he
did not even glance round him, but stood waiting unconcerned
for the tram, a man who did it every morning, reading the
doubled – over front page of the *Telegraaf* exactly like ten
thousand young men on their way to the office. Martin had a
horrid certainty that this was an entirely innocent person.

Sophia's elbow poked him nastily behind and her voice

murmured, 'Don't overact.'

'Is it him, do you think?'

'Of course, now shut up!' She stood at the edge of the pavement, and prodded with her umbrella at an empty cigarette carton. Clank clank went the approaching tram.

The young man went through to the back, a healthy tradition in the number four, whose front half has been known to fall in the Amstel – the nasty right-angled turn at the Half Maanstraat. Martin was not bothered about falling in the Amstel, but he went on through after him. It was already crowded, and he stood, three paces from the quarry. Quarry, he noticed with some satisfaction, had the nervous habit of lifting his eyes and glancing round, as though worried that the tram would go the wrong way. Martin hitched up against the partition, braced his feet apart against the bumpy crossing at the Frederiksplein, and pushed his hat back, staring innocently out of the window over quarry's head. Something registered, he could not quite see what; a fat woman was standing just between them. But at the Muntplein there was a scuffle to get out, and Martin noticed him make an irresolute move to follow at the last second.

'Make your mind up!' he said cheerfully, and caught a narrow, unsure glance.

All down the Rokin the glances kept flicking towards him and away; on the Damrak the quarry stood up. Martin was jostled by the fat woman. 'Umbrellas,' he said resignedly to the face looking straight into his. 'After you.' Quarry hared away at a great pace down towards the Stock Exchange. 'Is he really aiming to go into the Bijenkorf? – not possible; door's not open yet. He can't be making for the station; wouldn't have got out of the tram, or did he not guess I would follow?' As they reached the car park by the Beurs a black Mercedes slid in behind the row of taxis.

Berlage's Stock Exchange is a rather nasty *art nouveau* building which replaced a neo-classical horror. There is a popular Amsterdamse myth that there is a huge crack in the wall. Occasionally the city fathers are disposed to believe in this myth, but they have never had enough courage to knock the huge block down. Quarry hurried alongside it without stopping to hunt for the crack, and at the corner glanced back; Martin was doing an inexorable advance – no braces, no bowler, no pipe, tall, young and thin, but Maigret for all that. Quarry whipped round the corner.

He was gone when Martin reached it, giving Maigret a momentary shock before he thought of the public lavatory.

'Not much of a day,' he remarked brightly, busy with buttons. What would Sophia have done – admired the pretty boats in the basin? There she was indeed, like a tourist choosing between Kooi and Bergmann for a lovely ride in a waterbus. Quarry was scooting towards the Warmoesstraat. Was he going to make a call on a whore? No, he turned right, past the police bureau, back up towards the Dam. 'What's the daft fellow up to now?' thought Martin, quite breathless with the pace.

Opposite Krasnapolsky the sun had come out and the shops were taking down their shutters. Quarry turned into the Damstraat and went on down to the canal crossing, looking back at both corners. He hesitated before diving into the paper-shop on the corner, a deep narrow shop with a small front, sandwiched between cheap *kitsch* jewellery and souvenirs on one side and a fish-shop on the other. Martin breathed heavily – sharp sea-smell of shrimps – and wondered whether quarry had gone to ground. The street was full of students, hurrying to early lectures.

'Nice bit of eel for your sandwiches?' said the fishmonger's fat girl suddenly in his ear.

'Not those ones, Anneke, you've been playing with them.' Van der Valk's voice; coarse pleasantry. There was an exchange of vulgar Amsterdamse humour. Everything seemed swarming with life and colour; more like Naples than a northern city in mid-winter. Clunk chunk went the butcher's chopper opposite. The sun glinted on imitation silver spoons with town crests and portraits of the royal palace-on-the-Dam; somebody was yelling at a lorry-driver to get out of the way, and an English voice, terribly high pitched, said, 'My dear, do look'. Martin felt wildly excited.

Van der Valk looked about as excited as the palace-on-the-spoons, but had a satanic grin; Marquis di Gorgonzola, planning the white slave trade. 'All right; relax.'

'Does he work there, do you think?'

'We might as well take some fish; do you feel like eel?' Sophia, damned housewife.

'We'll soon know; I don't want you to chase in there. When Madame's got her fish – looks good, that eel – she can winkle him out if she likes. We've the time.'

'Shall I buy some papers?'

'That's the idea. Spend a few minutes and size him up. Probably waiting to see if a blockade forms outside, and killing time over a paperback. Good thing; makes him more nervous. Don't fluster him, just have a good look.'

'What did you think of the performance?' asked Martin.

'He's as cold as the cod there on the slab. Wanted to see if he was imagining things. We're on to the real thing all right. What he does next will clinch it.'

'What now?'

'Just wait first, for your wife. Keep out of sight; if he dodges out don't move till he begins to travel.'

Sophia was ten minutes before coming back happily with *Elle, Constanze, Margriet* and *Der Spiegel*, at which Martin raised his eyebrows.

'He works there; not the boss; just a counter-hand. The boss is a big fat man; do you know the place?'

'Not my territory; have to ask the boys in the Warmoesstraat.'

'It's the usual thing; loads of papers, German, American, everything; every magazine under the sun, postcards, paperbacks – what did strike me was it might be a good place to see naughty pictures.'

'Bit obvious, but it's well situated at that, just between the tourists and the old quarter. How many people work in the shop?'

'Just him and an old woman on the papers.'

'What about the fat man?'

'Gone. When I went in they were only just open and he was putting change in the cash register. Then he said something to our pal, and went out. Bank, maybe.'

'So there's only the boyfriend and an old woman. Like to try something? – you needn't if you don't want. Let's get off the street though, first.' He crossed the road and said a few words to Henk. 'There's a *kroeg* just along the road.'

There was nobody in the café but an obvious patronne, vigorously polishing the counter. She looked up in surprise. ''Morning, *'sieurs et dames*. My, my, you're really making a start.'

''Morning, patronne. Coffee brown yet?'

'*Verdorie*, the water isn't even on; I've only just had my tea – the cleaning isn't even done. Tell you what; I'll just dust the corner, and you can sit in peace, and I'll put the coffee on straight, if you don't mind waiting a tiny bit.'

Van der Valk leaned on the counter and gossiped familiarly till she had gone off cackling with laughter to get the coffee. He sat down then, produced his wallet full of pictures and handed it to Sophia. 'Henk will cover you in the shop; go back and say you've forgotten something. If you get the chance, bring these in – something like "A good friend told me about your pictures". If he reacts, make a date with him for this evening – say one of the cafés on the Voorburgwal – nowhere too crowded. How was he on the tram?'

'Once he saw me he couldn't keep still. He recognized me all right.'

'Good. Phase two is for Madame, whom he doesn't know, delicately to introduce the subject of photos.'

'What am I?' asked Sophia; 'wanting to buy or be bought?'

'I said delicately.' Van der Valk's grin was more like

Gorgonzola than ever. 'Being as delicate as I can, I think that if a policeman turns up breathing heavily the answer's a lemon, but a pretty girl looking for a job as a model might pick up more than a handful of gravel. Idea of this play-acting is to get him to admit he took the goddam photos.'

Martin stirred uneasily. 'I don't feel happy about her being alone with him.'

'This is no time to play the protective husband. Old quick-on-the-draw Henk is right behind her. You don't come on stage yet; anyway your wife's a good actress, and you're lousy.'

Sophia walked into the shop boldly, reassured by seeing a German tourist reading a little book about *la dolce vita* with apparent enjoyment. She went up to the young man, who was entering figures in a day book.

'I seem to have lost a glove and I was here earlier so I thought that maybe . . .'

'We'll look for you, Madame; whereabouts were you standing?'

Sophia leaned a little towards him with a lady-behind-the-window leer. 'My glove's in my pocket.'

The effect on his face was remarkable; he gave a quick uneasy look through the shop but said smoothly, 'I don't see how I can help you, Madame.'

'I'm from a good friend, who mentioned you to me. She had an accident –' The face was as tight shut as an oyster. A woman was standing waiting and he went to serve her. There was an involved story about a subscription. 'Now we'll see,' thought Sophia, picking up an *Elsevier*. 'If he's still interested that will clinch it.'

He finished with the woman and went to the German, who grinned and gibbered and waved his book.

'Take your time, *mein Herr*.' He went to the shop door and gave a sharp look from behind the tall rack of papers, up and down the street. Whatever he saw or didn't see, it seemed to reassure him. He came back towards Sophia with a rapid step. 'I'm sorry to keep you waiting, Madame,' loudly. 'I've had a good look for your glove, but . . .' The old woman was puzzling over a Swedish headline.

'How do I know you're from any friend?' he muttered, arranging the disordered magazines.

'She gave me something of yours. I can do some business with you, maybe.'

'What sort of business?'

'Photographic business. There's money in it.'

'Your friend isn't here to speak for herself.'

'No. She met an old boyfriend; ran into trouble.'

'She never mentioned it. Or you. Can you prove it?'

'Not in public, you fool. Still, just to show you I'm not kidding.' She flipped the top photo half out of the wallet and turned it towards him.

'She gave you those?'

'Lent them, to show some people in the business. She won't be needing them any more.'

'How long have you had them?'

Sophia felt she must push him harder. 'Look, mister, we're the ones who take the chances. You could be phony.'

Two men came in, one for *Yachting*, the other for the *Radio Engineers' Weekly*. He brought a notebook, and started listing the display. 'I have to see what to re-order. Who are these people you talk about?'

'Oh, art-dealers. Brussels, Antwerp, Paris. That's all you need know. The money talks.' The German was pottering towards them, smiling amiably.

'Can I meet you somewhere?' he said hurriedly. Sophia snatched the notebook and walked to the opposite wall.

'*Ein Gulden fünfundzwanzig. Precies. Vielen Dank. Wiedersehen, mein Herr.*' Le Château de Bordeaux, she wrote swiftly. Leliegracht. Seven tonight precisely.

'*Heer Je,*' said Van der Valk, 'you got pretty fancy. Still, that's what we want. We'll be keeping an eye on him.' He went to telephone. Henk came in with the suspicion of a grin.

'You went on a bit long, Madame, that was all. I had to interrupt; he would have thought up objections. Yes, my dear, I'd like a cup of coffee very much. How's the man? Still in bed, of course?' He sipped his coffee. 'We've got to get out of here. Where's Piet?'

'Telephone.'

Van der Valk reappeared, jaunty. 'All right, Madame, head for the car. Here's the keys. Henk, we're going to slip over to the Leliegracht. Now you,' to Martin, 'wait for me in the car.' Martin noticed the boxer strolling up the Damstraat.

'You told me not to overact,' he said rather crossly, getting in beside his wife.

'Possibly. But we know now, don't we?'

'Two gins with sugar and one with tonic,' ordered Van der Valk. 'This place will do nicely – seven in the evening there'll be no one here. I'll be at the table in the corner, Madame. This will be the clincher. All you have to do is give him the photos, really. Some story you want more copies; anything will do, just to tie him in. Then Martin here comes and sits with you; causes a big laugh. The only purpose in it is to knock him off balance a bit; I pinch him and he'll sing his head off. The two of you may as well go home. Big party tonight in the Leliegracht. I'll drive you back to pick up your car.'

Sophia had changed into a black frock that showed a good deal of bosom, and was brushing her hair. Martin's nervousness had made him disagreeable.

'I appreciate your dramatic success but don't get too carried away,' he said illogically. She looked at him thoughtfully, with the brush making automatic sweeps at the back of her neck.

'Come here. I want to tell you something.'

'What? Hurry up, we haven't all day.'

'Do you want to make love to me now or later? Go on, do it now, and afterwards you can hire me a window in the Oude-kerkplein. Come over here, *sufferd*.'

'Don't drink too much, and don't join me for a quarter of an hour anyway. He may be late, and I have to get him to the right point anyway.' They were parked under trees at the corner of the Herengracht. 'And get away from here; anyone coming from the Dam side would see you.'

'*Ciaou* then.'

The Château de Bordeaux is a bar with a pleasant atmosphere. They have good wine from the wood. There is nothing French about the interior; it is plainly Dutch – *rotan* furniture and Heineken beer-mats. There are no log fires, and not even a neon outside. But there is an admirable pianist, the wine and the coffee are both good, and the atmosphere stays fresh however many cigars are smoked. The *castelein* is French; he comes from the Charente and always has good Zeeland oysters; he makes *mouclade* too. Everything is as it should be. He has two French-speaking barmaids in big linen aprons, and Madame; she is Friesian, and wears a golden helmet, which seems illogical; she is tall, blonde, and has an excellent business brain.

The young man was sitting in the corner, over the far side from where Van der Valk and the boxer were drinking hot wine with a smell of cinnamon and orange peel. He had a beer in front of him, and looked none too happy. After shutting the shop he had not gone home, but had tacked all round the town to make sure he was not being followed. He had been too nervous to eat, but had had a beer in the Zeedijk, another in the Haarlemmerstraat, and another in the Hugo de Groot. He had been all round the centre of the town, was cold, tired and a bit drunk, but felt a great deal better now that he was quite certain that nobody had followed him. The boxer was telling Van der Valk all about this when Sophia came in.

She sat down opposite him, from where she could see the whole room. He did not stand up. 'Peasant' she thought. 'Did Elsa teach you no manners then?' One of the girls came for her order, and she asked for cognac, and joked in French over the spirit-lamp. The young man evidently knew no French; he

187

was out of his depth and looked uneasy. She saw she had made an error, opened her coat, and let him have a good look at her throat. The cognac was very good; she felt confident and calm. Once he had seen her dress he got less down in the mouth; even paying for the cognac was less of a disaster.

'Now, let's get to business. These photos are pretty good; you're smart at that.' A small smile, self-satisfied. 'Any more you take for us, it's two hundred fifty guilder a time.' His eyes opened wider. 'You can hire a studio, somewhere quiet.'

'Who could I take photos of?'

'Not the shits along the Achterburgwal. But I'll take care of that end of it. Here, you'd better have these back for the present; we'll be wanting a few copies of them.'

His eyes showed the extent of his relief. 'You know the police were in her flat only a day or so ago.'

'You've nothing to worry about now that you've got these back.'

He leaned back and called the waitress, ordered two more cognacs. When his came he drank it straight off. 'That's better. It's cold, but I'm beginning to warm up.'

She gave him a sweet smile. 'In this business that's what we drink.'

'I don't drink much.' His voice had got hoarse. 'Tell me,' he leaned forward, eyes fixed a little glassily on her throat, 'could I take some photos of you?'

She drank half her second cognac with her eyes shut before managing another beaming smile.

'You'll have to take me somewhere good to dinner first. Anyway I'm going to have another drink.' She breathed in the perfume of her glass, watching him, thinking. *'Tiens, tiens; never knew myself capable'*. A hand drew out the chair alongside her and Martin's voice, jovial, rather ginny, said, 'Good evening, all.'

The young man was more than half drunk; the warmth and the generous brandy on top of cold, hunger and four beers had kicked him in the face. His nose got putty-coloured;

188

sweat showed all along his forehead. He stared at Martin, with a fixed, half stupid smile that suddenly reminded Sophia of Elsa's expression, on the photographs that were safely in his pocket.

'Who . . . who . . . ?'

'Sure, that's right. This morning in the tram. Last seen one night out of the window, in the Josef Israelskade. And once, I think, in the Kalverstraat.'

The eyes dragged round to Sophia.

'Do you know this man?' The eyes begged for help.

'Certainly I do. He is my husband.'

Martin leaned forward and said viciously, 'You made a sweet job of killing her, didn't you?'

The eyes had gone out of focus; with a jump the young man was on his feet and backing away. Something from Martin's army days had him standing in the same instant. The young man had a gun in his hand, and seemed unsure which of the two to aim at. Van der Valk grabbed for the ashtray; it hit the shoulder-blade but was not heavy enough; he lunged for his own gun. Martin's action was unthinking. Swinging the *rotan* chair up with both hands, he put his head down and charged. He heard the two shots, in the same instant felt the chair go home on its target, and then he was sprawling on the floor with half the breath knocked out of him.

Powerful hand lifted his shoulders and turned him. He blinked; the doggy brown eyes of the boxer were looking in his.

'Hit at all?'

'Don't know; don't think so.' There was a dead silence.

'Police,' said Van der Valk in his circular-saw voice. 'Quiet and still; it's all over. Telephone, quick.'

Martin could hear the bump and ting on the bar, the thrash of the dial.

'Van der Valk. Emergency. Ambulance. French wine shop on the Leliegracht, and make it fast.' Martin was on his feet with a stagger and a pain in the ankle. He looked down; blood was trickling between his shoe and his trouser cuff.

'Sophia!' he yelped.

Van der Valk, at the bar, looked as though carved from the same piece of teak. 'Shut up. Nothing hit her.'

She was standing by the table. Madame, one arm protectively round her and the coppery lamplight glinting on the golden helmet, was holding the brandy glass. There was the sharp smell of the shots stinging in his nose, so that he wanted to sneeze; he yawned instead, nervously. Another smell, this one like the Quai de Bercy. Jeanjean, the *castelein,* had had the same idea as Van der Valk, and had thrown the first thing that came to hand, a bottle three-quarters full of red Bordeaux. It had hit Martin's chair, and splintered on the wall beyond.

'Take it easy everyone,' said Van der Valk calmly to the room. 'It's quite finished.'

'Died. On the way to the Binnen Gasthuis, in the ambulance. I got him in the lung as you knocked him silly into the wall. Violent haemorrhage. I had to shoot, the gun was on your wife; you took him though, *jongen.*' There was a certain respect in the policeman's voice. 'He's in the mortuary now, where you saw her last. Be a good joke,' with a return of his old brutal humour, 'if he was in the same compartment . . . It's all got the string tied round already. I hadn't foreseen the gun, *sufferd* that I am; I'm sure as hell going to have a time explaining this to the examining magistrate.'

'Are you going to take that nembutal?' asked Sophia.

'I've already taken it. Darling I love you.'

'Yes. I love you. Sleep quietly, I'm holding you.'

'All done by love, as usual,' said Mr Slotemaker de Bruin, mildly.

'Yes,' answered Van der Valk, relieved enough to risk a joke. 'Here in Amsterdam love causes the police no end of trouble.'

More about Penguins

Penguinews, which appears every month, contains details of all the new books issued by Penguins as they are published. From time to time it is supplemented by *Penguins in Print*, which is a complete list of all available books published by Penguins. (There are some five thousand of these.)

A specimen copy of *Penguinews* will be sent to you free on request. For a year's issues (including the complete lists) please send 50p if you live in the British Isles, or 75p if you live elsewhere. Just write to Dept EP, Penguin Books Ltd, Harmondsworth, Middlesex, enclosing a cheque or postal order, and your name will be added to the mailing list.

In the U.S.A.: For a complete list of books available from Penguin in the United States write to Dept CS, Penguin Books Inc., 7110 Ambassador Road, Baltimore, Maryland 21207.

In Canada: For a complete list of books available from Penguin in Canada write to Penguin Books Canada Ltd, 41 Steelcase Road West, Markham, Ontario.

Nicolas Freeling

'My whole idea,' states one of Freeling's characters, 'was to write about Europe in a European idiom. Something that has a European flavour and inflection.' If this was also Nicolas Freeling's intention, what a triumphant start he has made to his un-American activities! Here are characters that are subtle rather than tough; dialogue that echoes real life; settings (in the Low Countries) exactly inventoried; and, in Van der Valk, the Dutch inspector, a detective as human and unorthodox as Maigret himself.

'Has established himself as the most interesting new crime writer for some years' – Maurice Richardson in the *Observer*

The following novels are also available:

Because of the Cats
Criminal Conversation *
Double-Barrel
Gun Before Butter *
The King of the Rainy Country
This is the Castle *
Tsing-Boum *
Valparaiso *

* Not for sale in the U.S.A.